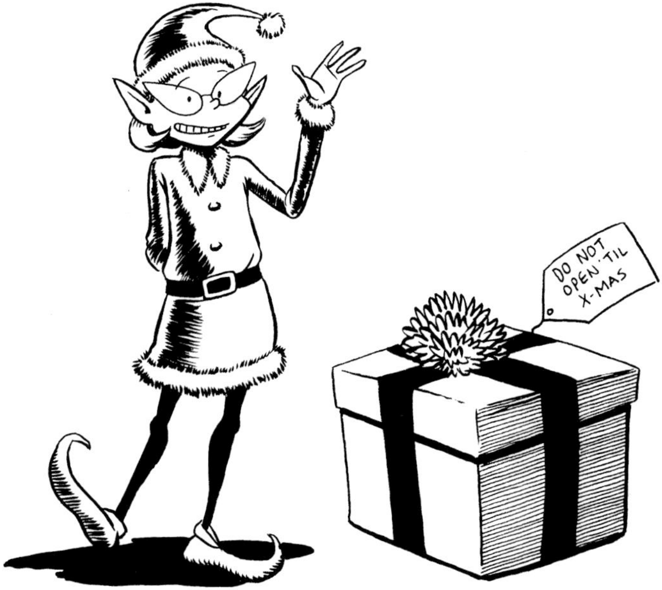
DO NOT
OPEN 'TIL
X-MAS

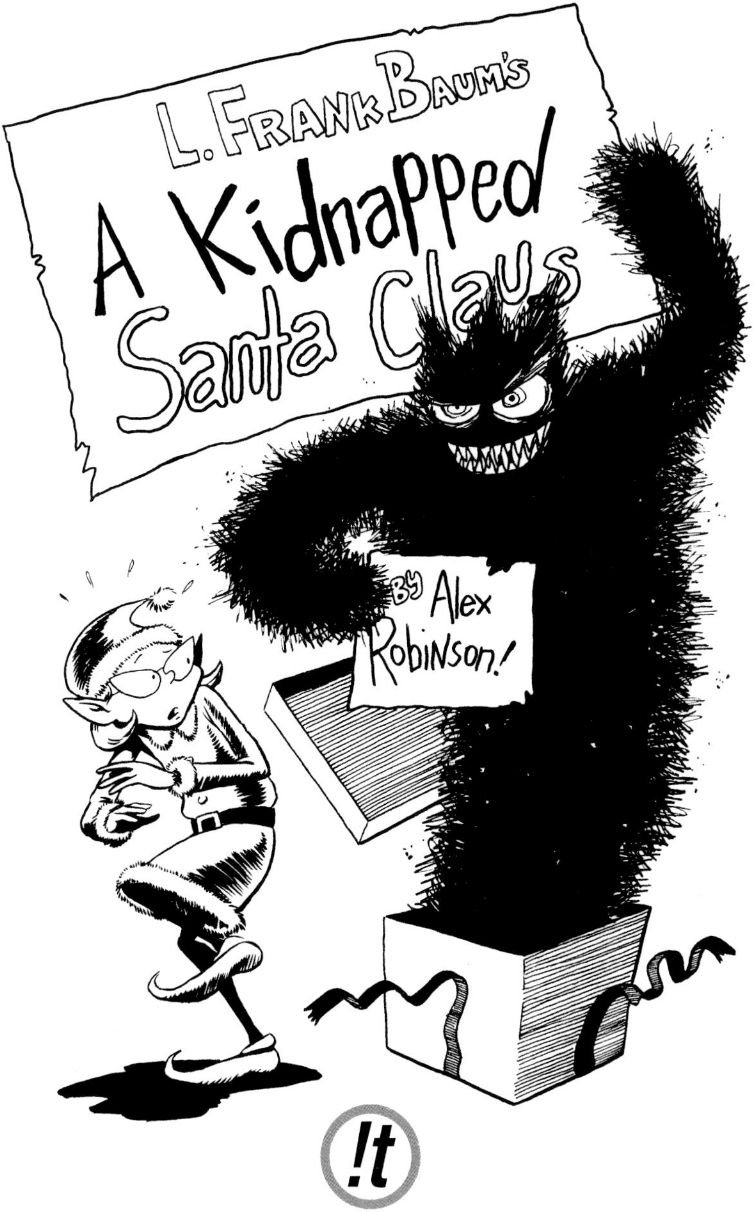
L. Frank Baum's
A Kidnapped Santa Claus
By Alex Robinson!

itbooks
AN IMPRINT OF HARPERCOLLINSPUBLISHERS

A KIDNAPPED SANTA CLAUS. Copyright © 2009 by Alex Robinson. All rights
reserved. Printed in China. No part of this book may be used or reproduced in
any manner whatsoever without written permission except in the case of brief
quotations embodied in critical articles and reviews. For information address
HarperCollins Publishers, 10 East 53rd Street, New York, NY 10022.

HarperCollins books may be purchased for educational, business, or sales
promotional use. For information please write: Special Markets Department,
HarperCollins Publishers, 10 East 53rd Street, New York, NY 10022.

FIRST EDITION

ISBN 978-0-06-178240-4

09   10   11   12   13   10   9   8   7   6   5   4   3   2   1

SANTA CLAUS LIVES IN THE LAUGHING VALLEY IN A BIG RAMBLING CASTLE. HIS WORKERS ALL LIVE WITH HIM AND EVERYONE IS AS BUSY AS CAN BE FROM ONE YEAR'S END TO ANOTHER!

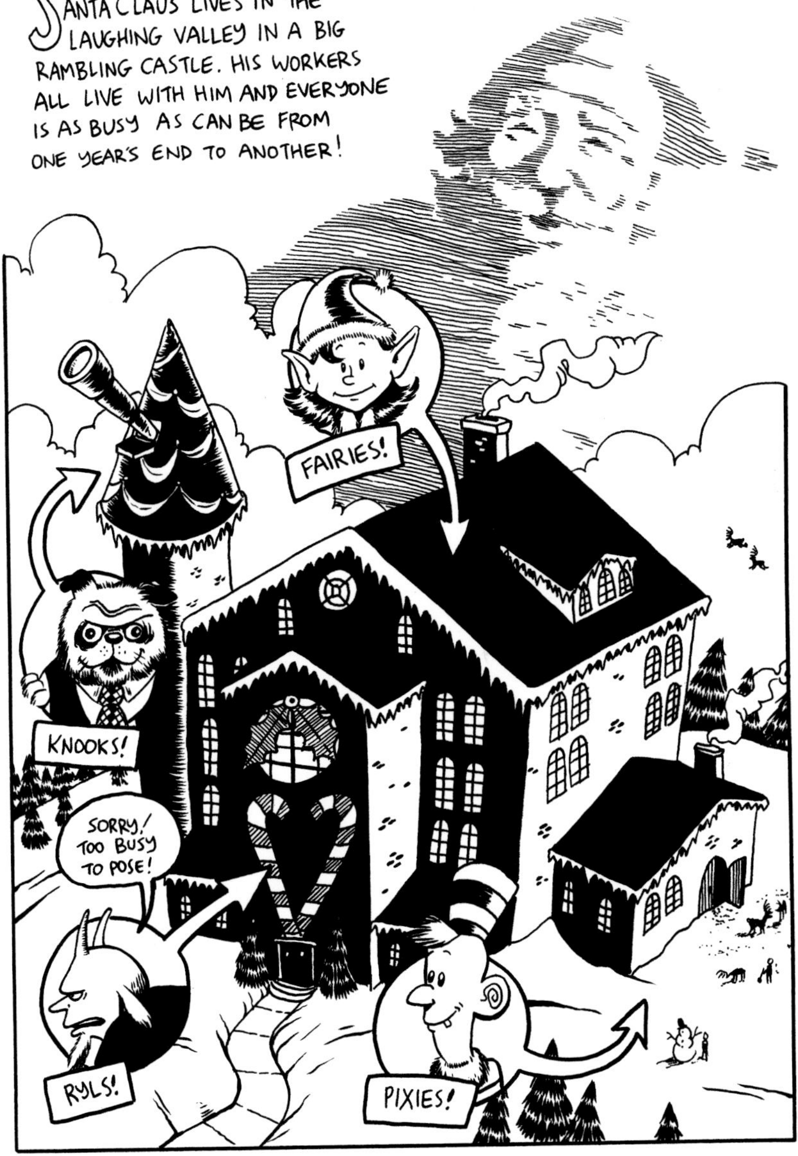
FAIRIES!
KNOOKS!
SORRY! TOO BUSY TO POSE!
RYLS!
PIXIES!

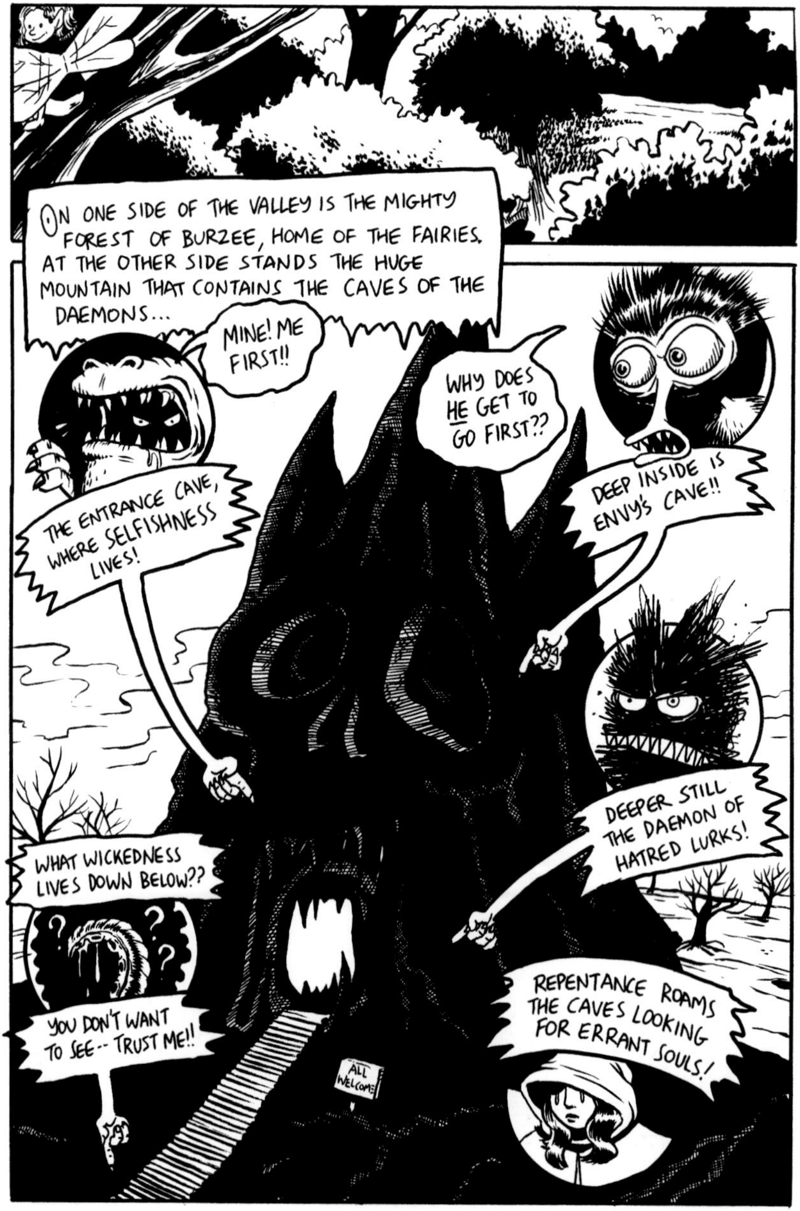
ON ONE SIDE OF THE VALLEY IS THE MIGHTY FOREST OF BURZEE, HOME OF THE FAIRIES. AT THE OTHER SIDE STANDS THE HUGE MOUNTAIN THAT CONTAINS THE CAVES OF THE DAEMONS...
MINE! ME FIRST!!
WHY DOES HE GET TO GO FIRST??
THE ENTRANCE CAVE, WHERE SELFISHNESS LIVES!
DEEP INSIDE IS ENVY'S CAVE!!
DEEPER STILL THE DAEMON OF HATRED LURKS!
WHAT WICKEDNESS LIVES DOWN BELOW??
YOU DON'T WANT TO SEE-- TRUST ME!!
ALL WELCOME
REPENTANCE ROAMS THE CAVES LOOKING FOR ERRANT SOULS!

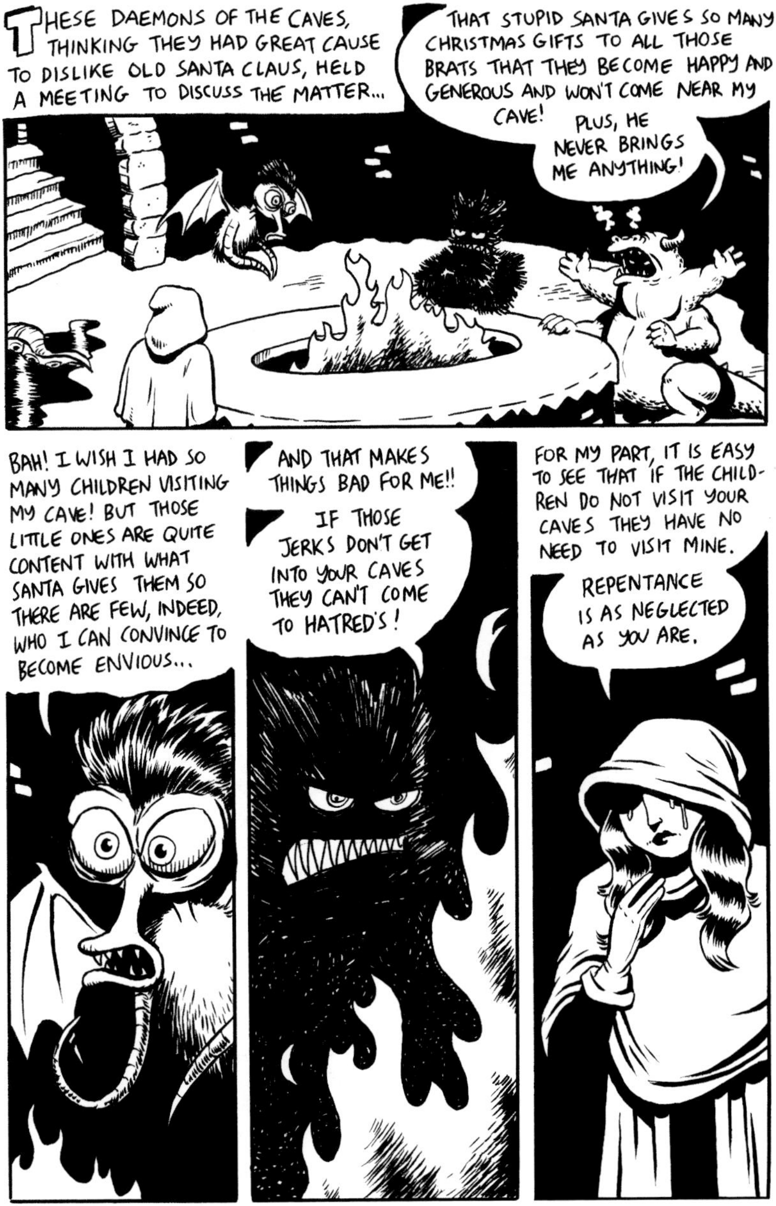
THESE DAEMONS OF THE CAVES, THINKING THEY HAD GREAT CAUSE TO DISLIKE OLD SANTA CLAUS, HELD A MEETING TO DISCUSS THE MATTER...
THAT STUPID SANTA GIVES SO MANY CHRISTMAS GIFTS TO ALL THOSE BRATS THAT THEY BECOME HAPPY AND GENEROUS AND WON'T COME NEAR MY CAVE!
PLUS, HE NEVER BRINGS ME ANYTHING!
BAH! I WISH I HAD SO MANY CHILDREN VISITING MY CAVE! BUT THOSE LITTLE ONES ARE QUITE CONTENT WITH WHAT SANTA GIVES THEM SO THERE ARE FEW, INDEED, WHO I CAN CONVINCE TO BECOME ENVIOUS...
AND THAT MAKES THINGS BAD FOR ME!!
IF THOSE JERKS DON'T GET INTO YOUR CAVES THEY CAN'T COME TO HATRED'S!
FOR MY PART, IT IS EASY TO SEE THAT IF THE CHILDREN DO NOT VISIT YOUR CAVES THEY HAVE NO NEED TO VISIT MINE.
REPENTANCE IS AS NEGLECTED AS YOU ARE.

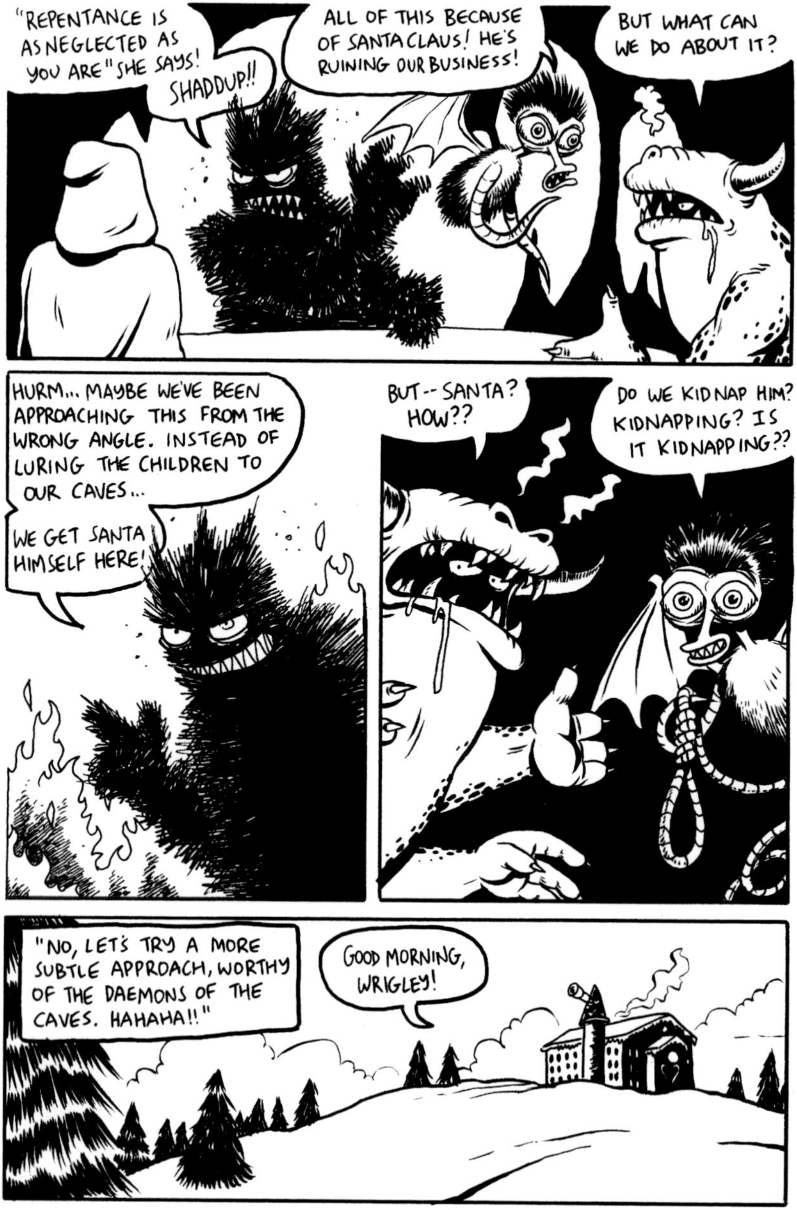
"REPENTANCE IS AS NEGLECTED AS YOU ARE" SHE SAYS!
SHADDUP!!
ALL OF THIS BECAUSE OF SANTA CLAUS! HE'S RUINING OUR BUSINESS!
BUT WHAT CAN WE DO ABOUT IT?
HURM... MAYBE WE'VE BEEN APPROACHING THIS FROM THE WRONG ANGLE. INSTEAD OF LURING THE CHILDREN TO OUR CAVES...
WE GET SANTA HIMSELF HERE!
BUT--SANTA? HOW??
DO WE KIDNAP HIM? KIDNAPPING? IS IT KIDNAPPING??
"NO, LET'S TRY A MORE SUBTLE APPROACH, WORTHY OF THE DAEMONS OF THE CAVES. HAHAHA!!"
GOOD MORNING, WRIGLEY!

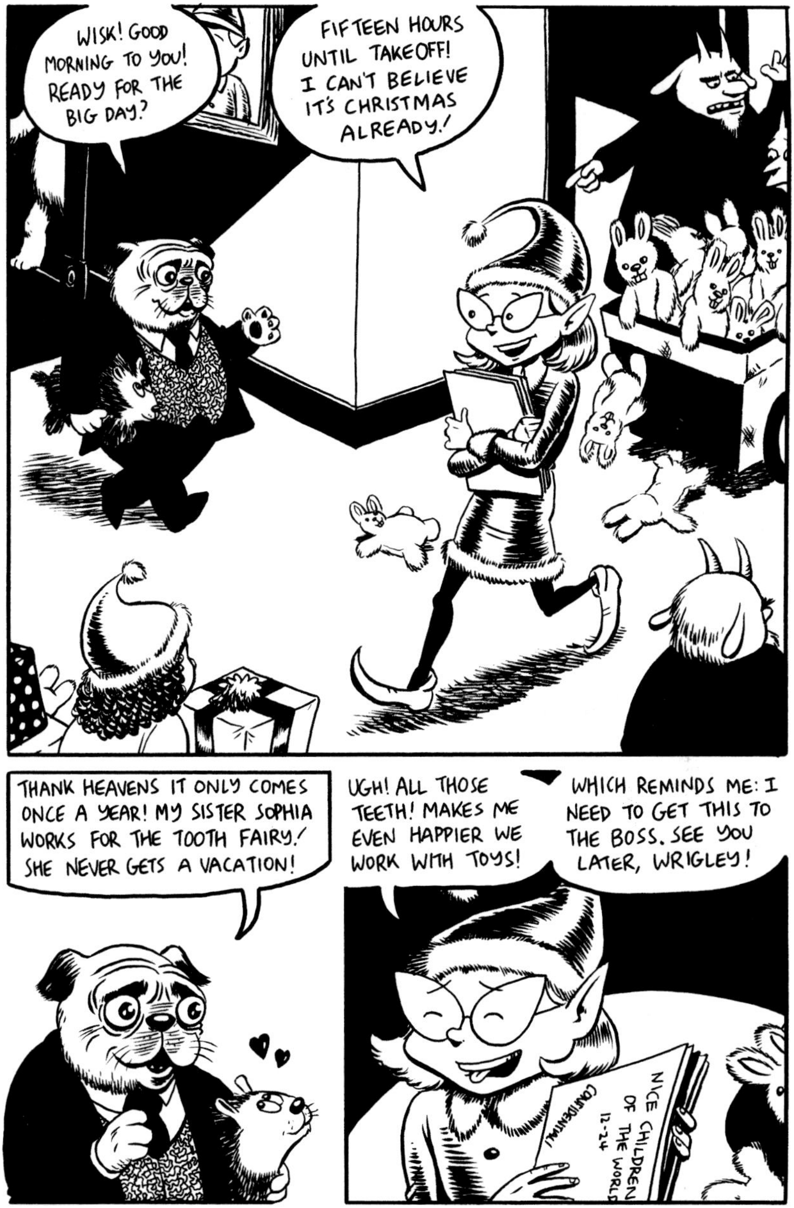
WISK! GOOD MORNING TO YOU! READY FOR THE BIG DAY?
FIFTEEN HOURS UNTIL TAKEOFF! I CAN'T BELIEVE IT'S CHRISTMAS ALREADY!
THANK HEAVENS IT ONLY COMES ONCE A YEAR! MY SISTER SOPHIA WORKS FOR THE TOOTH FAIRY! SHE NEVER GETS A VACATION!
UGH! ALL THOSE TEETH! MAKES ME EVEN HAPPIER WE WORK WITH TOYS!
WHICH REMINDS ME: I NEED TO GET THIS TO THE BOSS. SEE YOU LATER, WRIGLEY!
NICE CHILDREN OF THE WORLD
12-24
CONFIDENTIAL!

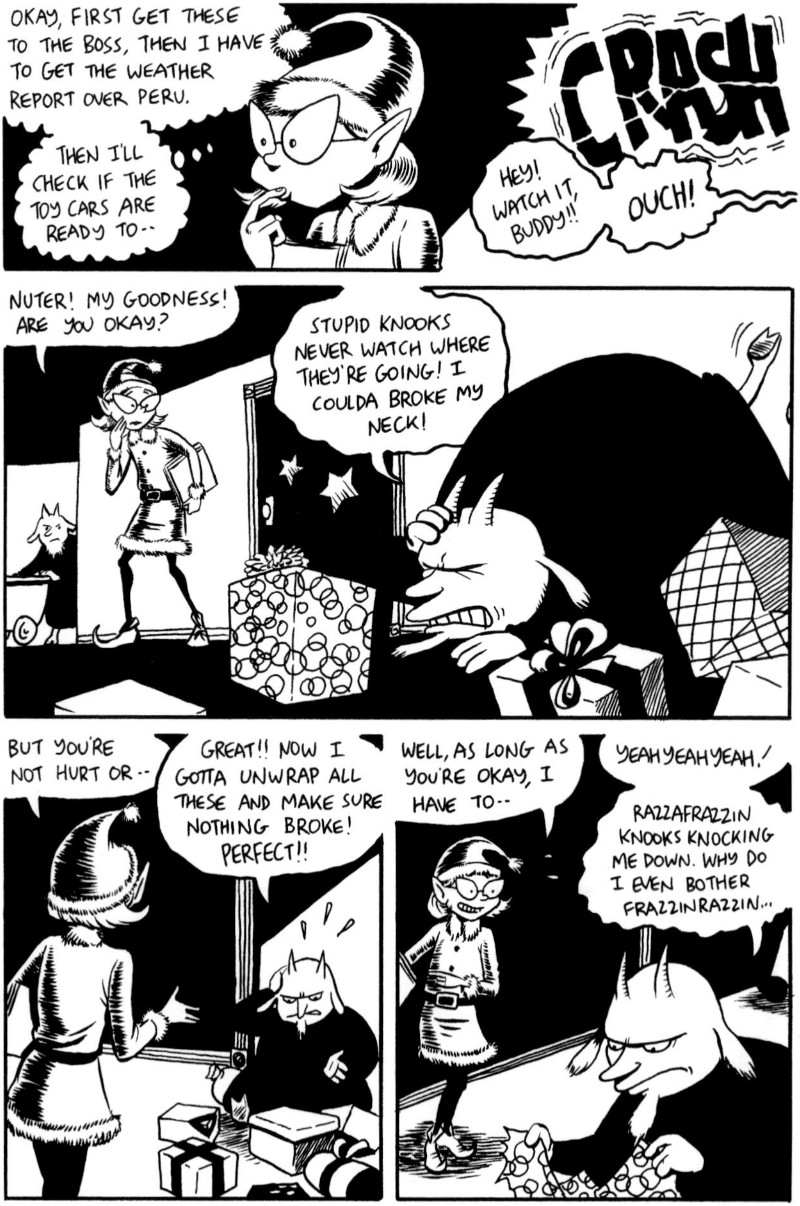
OKAY, FIRST GET THESE TO THE BOSS, THEN I HAVE TO GET THE WEATHER REPORT OVER PERU.
THEN I'LL CHECK IF THE TOY CARS ARE READY TO--
CRASH
HEY! WATCH IT, BUDDY!!
OUCH!
NUTER! MY GOODNESS! ARE YOU OKAY?
STUPID KNOOKS NEVER WATCH WHERE THEY'RE GOING! I COULDA BROKE MY NECK!
BUT YOU'RE NOT HURT OR--
GREAT!! NOW I GOTTA UNWRAP ALL THESE AND MAKE SURE NOTHING BROKE! PERFECT!!
WELL, AS LONG AS YOU'RE OKAY, I HAVE TO--
YEAHYEAHYEAH!
RAZZAFRAZZIN KNOOKS KNOCKING ME DOWN. WHY DO I EVEN BOTHER FRAZZINRAZZIN...

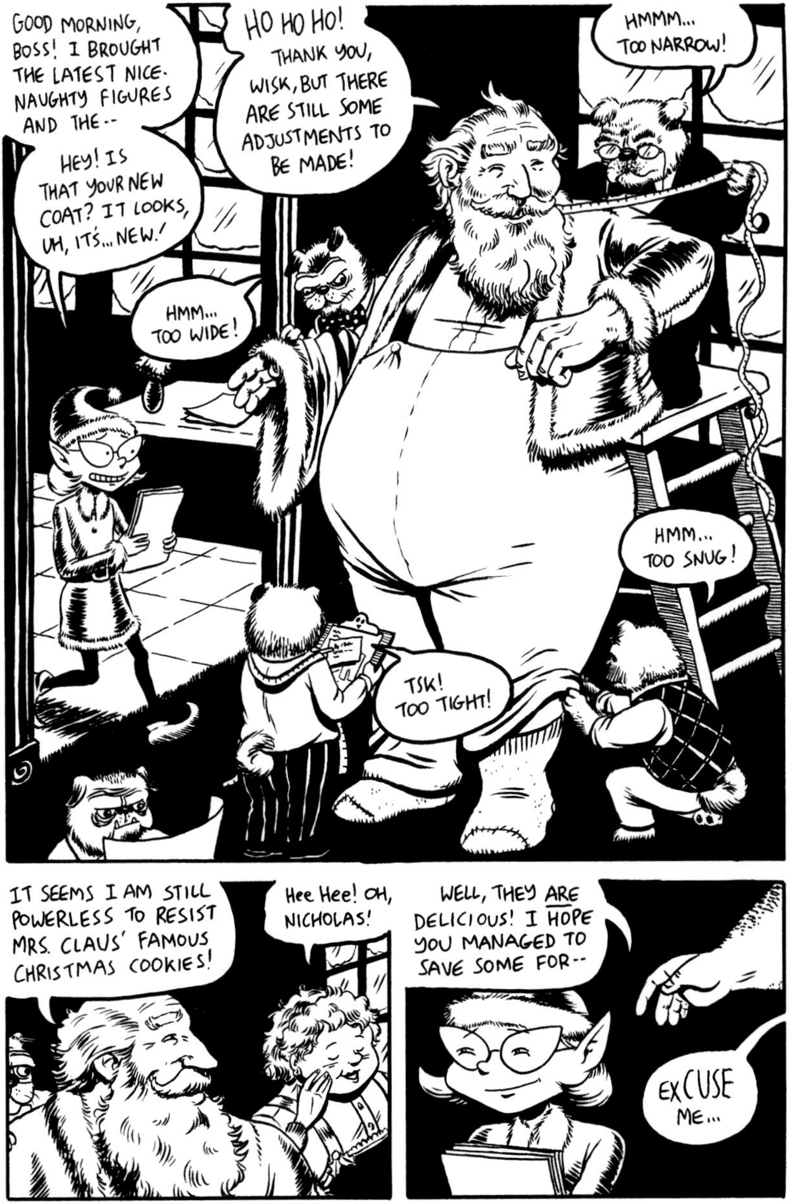
GOOD MORNING, BOSS! I BROUGHT THE LATEST NICE-NAUGHTY FIGURES AND THE--
HO HO HO! THANK YOU, WISK, BUT THERE ARE STILL SOME ADJUSTMENTS TO BE MADE!
HEY! IS THAT YOUR NEW COAT? IT LOOKS, UH, IT'S... NEW!
HMMM... TOO NARROW!
HMM... TOO WIDE!
HMM... TOO SNUG!
TSK! TOO TIGHT!
IT SEEMS I AM STILL POWERLESS TO RESIST MRS. CLAUS' FAMOUS CHRISTMAS COOKIES!
Hee Hee! OH, NICHOLAS!
WELL, THEY ARE DELICIOUS! I HOPE YOU MANAGED TO SAVE SOME FOR--
EXCUSE ME...

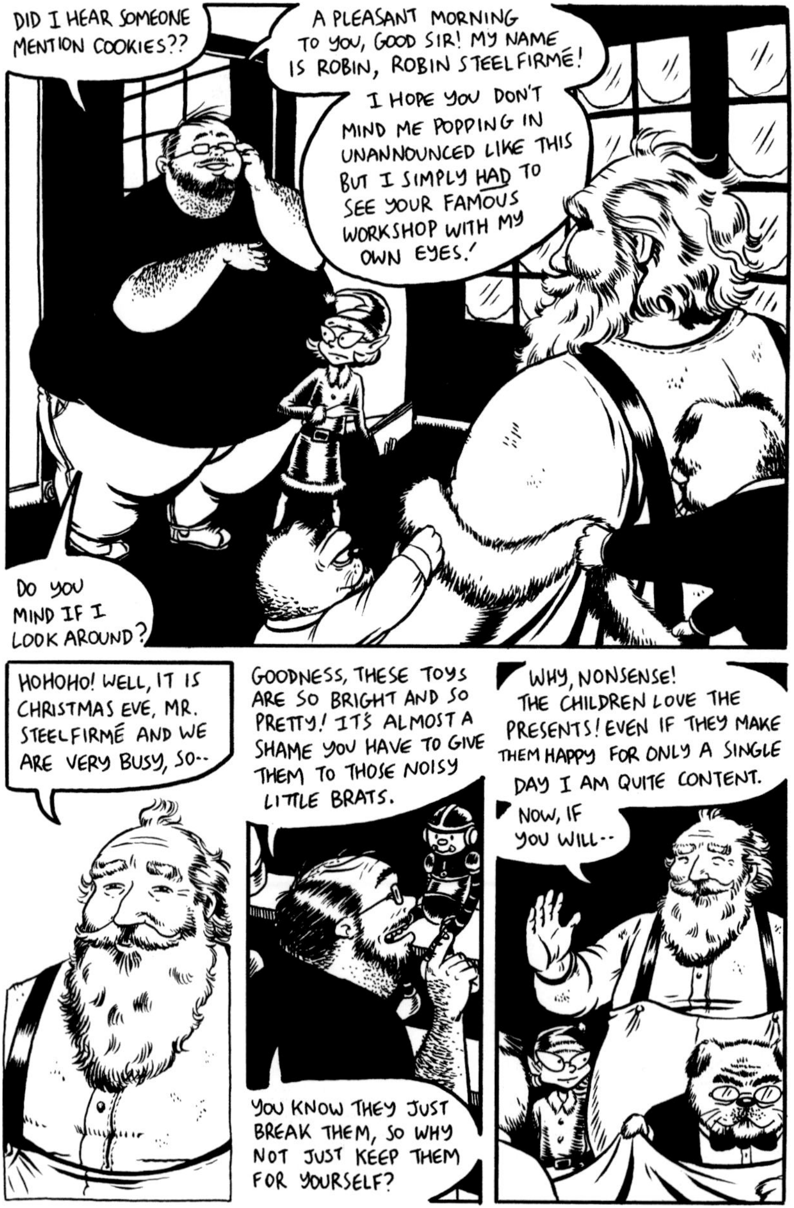
DID I HEAR SOMEONE MENTION COOKIES??
A PLEASANT MORNING TO YOU, GOOD SIR! MY NAME IS ROBIN, ROBIN STEELFIRMÉ!
I HOPE YOU DON'T MIND ME POPPING IN UNANNOUNCED LIKE THIS BUT I SIMPLY HAD TO SEE YOUR FAMOUS WORKSHOP WITH MY OWN EYES!
DO YOU MIND IF I LOOK AROUND?
HOHOHO! WELL, IT IS CHRISTMAS EVE, MR. STEELFIRMÉ AND WE ARE VERY BUSY, SO--
GOODNESS, THESE TOYS ARE SO BRIGHT AND SO PRETTY! IT'S ALMOST A SHAME YOU HAVE TO GIVE THEM TO THOSE NOISY LITTLE BRATS.
YOU KNOW THEY JUST BREAK THEM, SO WHY NOT JUST KEEP THEM FOR YOURSELF?
WHY, NONSENSE! THE CHILDREN LOVE THE PRESENTS! EVEN IF THEY MAKE THEM HAPPY FOR ONLY A SINGLE DAY I AM QUITE CONTENT.
NOW, IF YOU WILL--

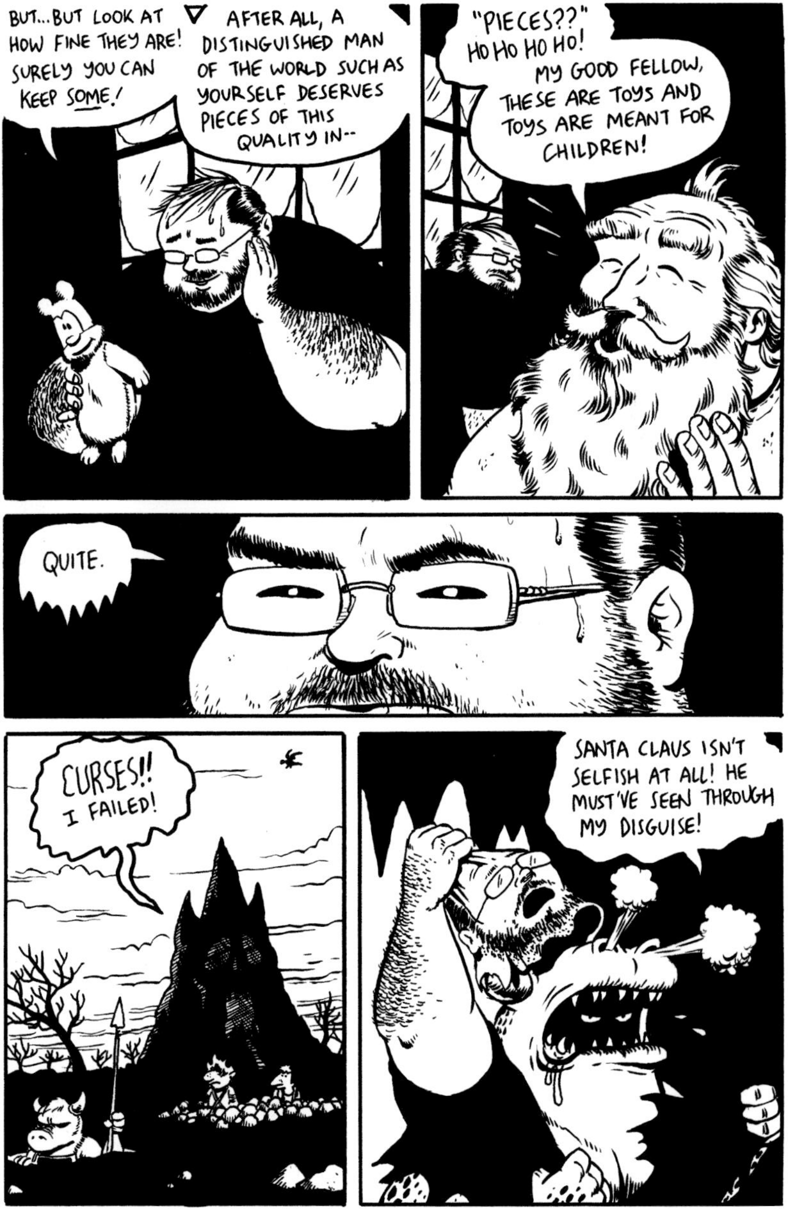
BUT...BUT LOOK AT HOW FINE THEY ARE! SURELY YOU CAN KEEP SOME!
AFTER ALL, A DISTINGUISHED MAN OF THE WORLD SUCH AS YOURSELF DESERVES PIECES OF THIS QUALITY IN--
"PIECES??" HO HO HO HO!
MY GOOD FELLOW, THESE ARE TOYS AND TOYS ARE MEANT FOR CHILDREN!
QUITE.
CURSES!! I FAILED!
SANTA CLAUS ISN'T SELFISH AT ALL! HE MUST'VE SEEN THROUGH MY DISGUISE!

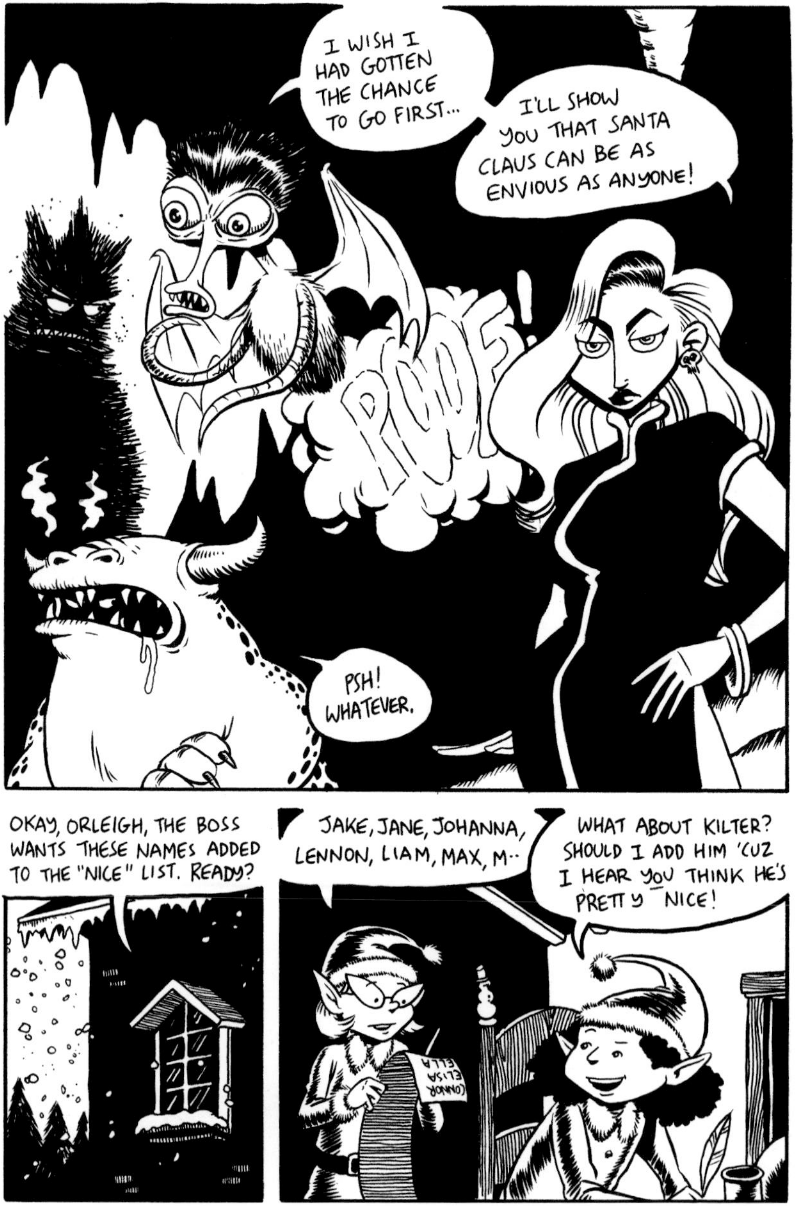

I WISH I HAD GOTTEN THE CHANCE TO GO FIRST...
I'LL SHOW YOU THAT SANTA CLAUS CAN BE AS ENVIOUS AS ANYONE!
POOF!
PSH! WHATEVER.
OKAY, ORLEIGH, THE BOSS WANTS THESE NAMES ADDED TO THE "NICE" LIST. READY?
JAKE, JANE, JOHANNA, LENNON, LIAM, MAX, M··
WHAT ABOUT KILTER? SHOULD I ADD HIM 'CUZ I HEAR YOU THINK HE'S PRETTY NICE!

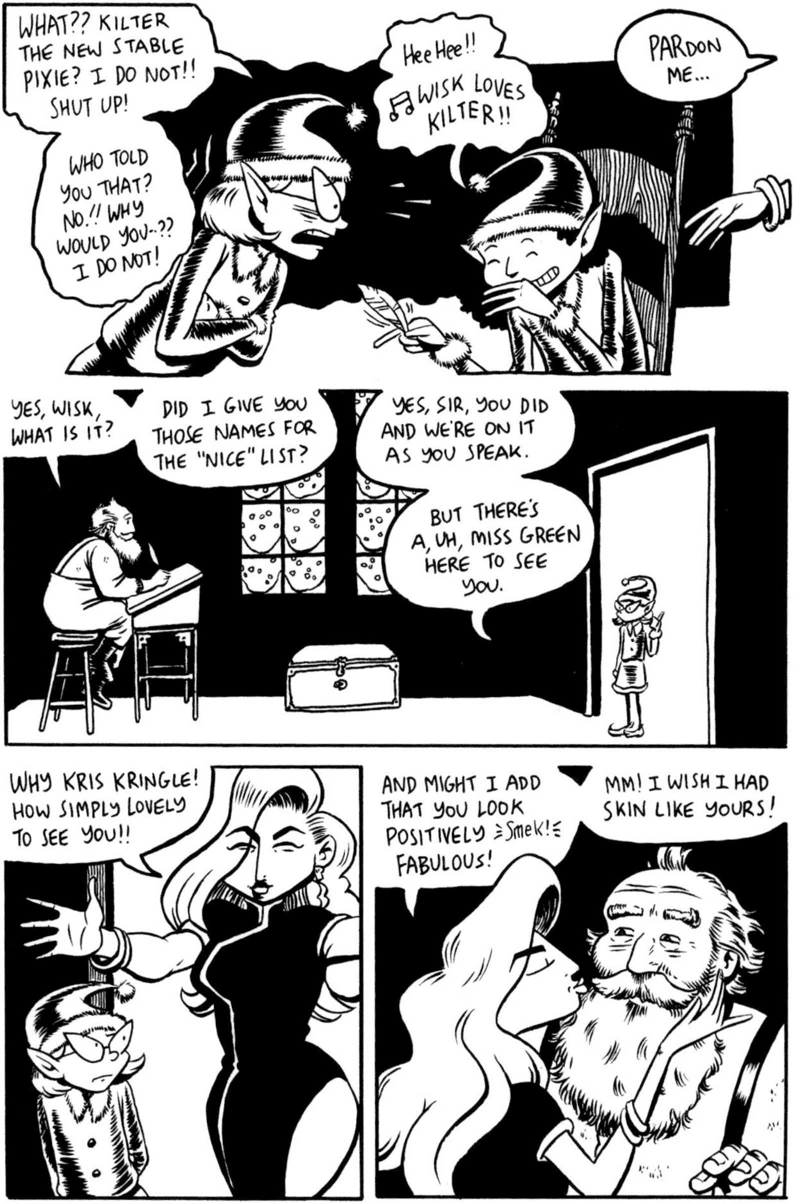
WHAT?? KILTER THE NEW STABLE PIXIE? I DO NOT!! SHUT UP!
WHO TOLD YOU THAT? NO.!! WHY WOULD YOU-.?? I DO NOT!
Hee Hee!!
♫ WISK LOVES KILTER!!
PARDON ME...
YES, WISK, WHAT IS IT?
DID I GIVE YOU THOSE NAMES FOR THE "NICE" LIST?
YES, SIR, YOU DID AND WE'RE ON IT AS YOU SPEAK.
BUT THERE'S A, UH, MISS GREEN HERE TO SEE YOU.
WHY KRIS KRINGLE! HOW SIMPLY LOVELY TO SEE YOU!!
AND MIGHT I ADD THAT YOU LOOK POSITIVELY ≷Smek!≶ FABULOUS!
MM! I WISH I HAD SKIN LIKE YOURS!

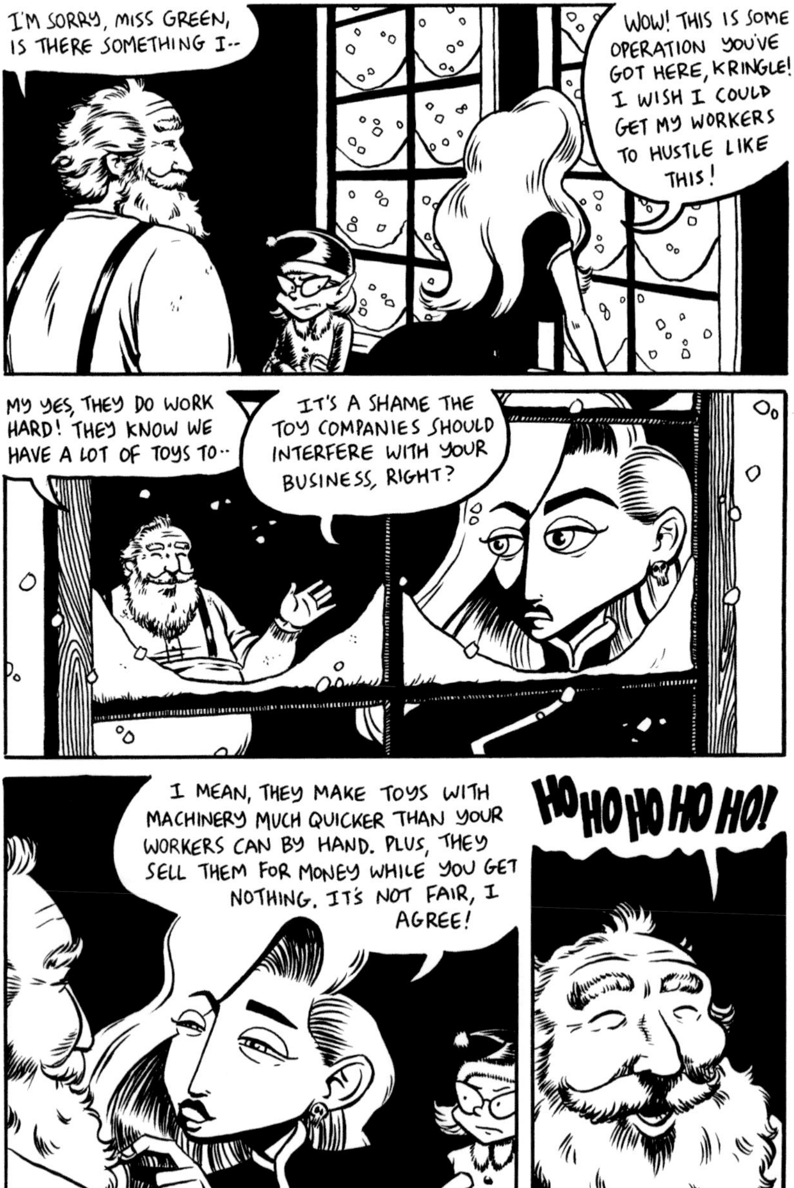
I'M SORRY, MISS GREEN, IS THERE SOMETHING I--
WOW! THIS IS SOME OPERATION YOU'VE GOT HERE, KRINGLE! I WISH I COULD GET MY WORKERS TO HUSTLE LIKE THIS!
MY YES, THEY DO WORK HARD! THEY KNOW WE HAVE A LOT OF TOYS TO..
IT'S A SHAME THE TOY COMPANIES SHOULD INTERFERE WITH YOUR BUSINESS, RIGHT?
I MEAN, THEY MAKE TOYS WITH MACHINERY MUCH QUICKER THAN YOUR WORKERS CAN BY HAND. PLUS, THEY SELL THEM FOR MONEY WHILE YOU GET NOTHING. IT'S NOT FAIR, I AGREE!
HO HO HO HO HO!

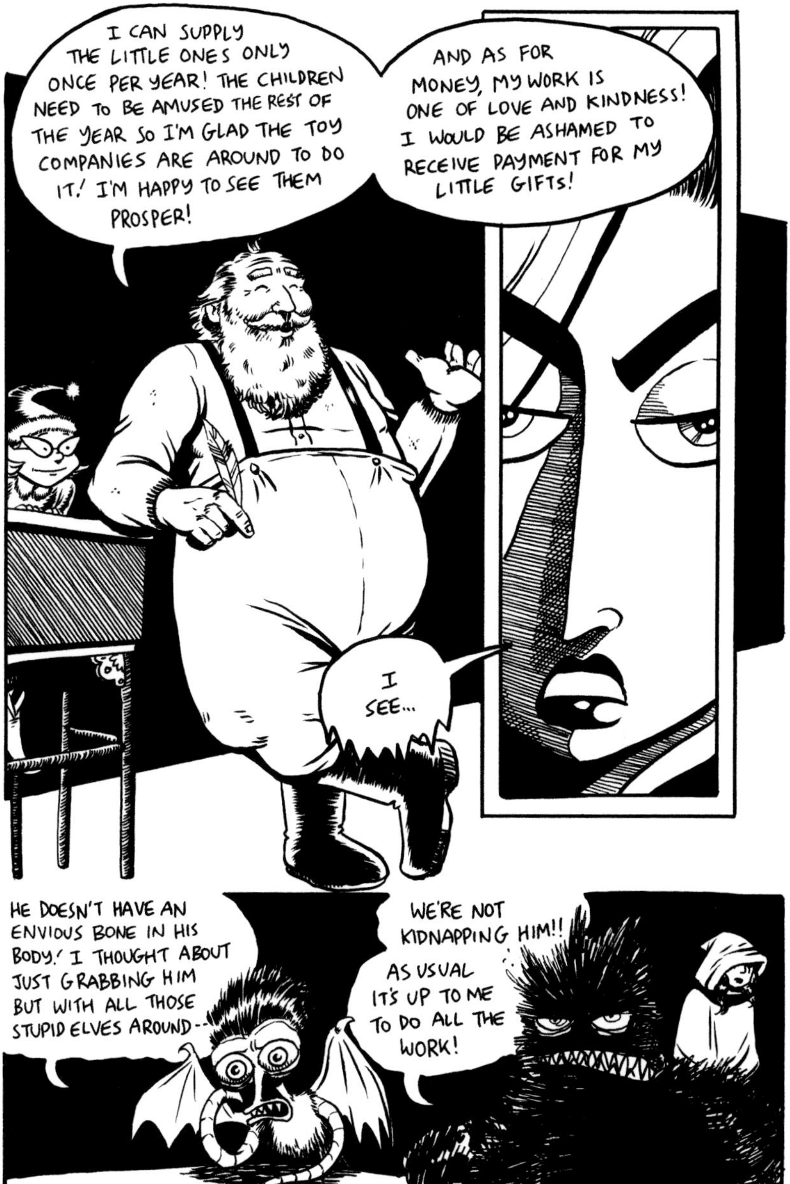
I CAN SUPPLY THE LITTLE ONES ONLY ONCE PER YEAR! THE CHILDREN NEED TO BE AMUSED THE REST OF THE YEAR SO I'M GLAD THE TOY COMPANIES ARE AROUND TO DO IT! I'M HAPPY TO SEE THEM PROSPER!
AND AS FOR MONEY, MY WORK IS ONE OF LOVE AND KINDNESS! I WOULD BE ASHAMED TO RECEIVE PAYMENT FOR MY LITTLE GIFTS!
I SEE...
HE DOESN'T HAVE AN ENVIOUS BONE IN HIS BODY! I THOUGHT ABOUT JUST GRABBING HIM BUT WITH ALL THOSE STUPID ELVES AROUND--
WE'RE NOT KIDNAPPING HIM!!
AS USUAL IT'S UP TO ME TO DO ALL THE WORK!

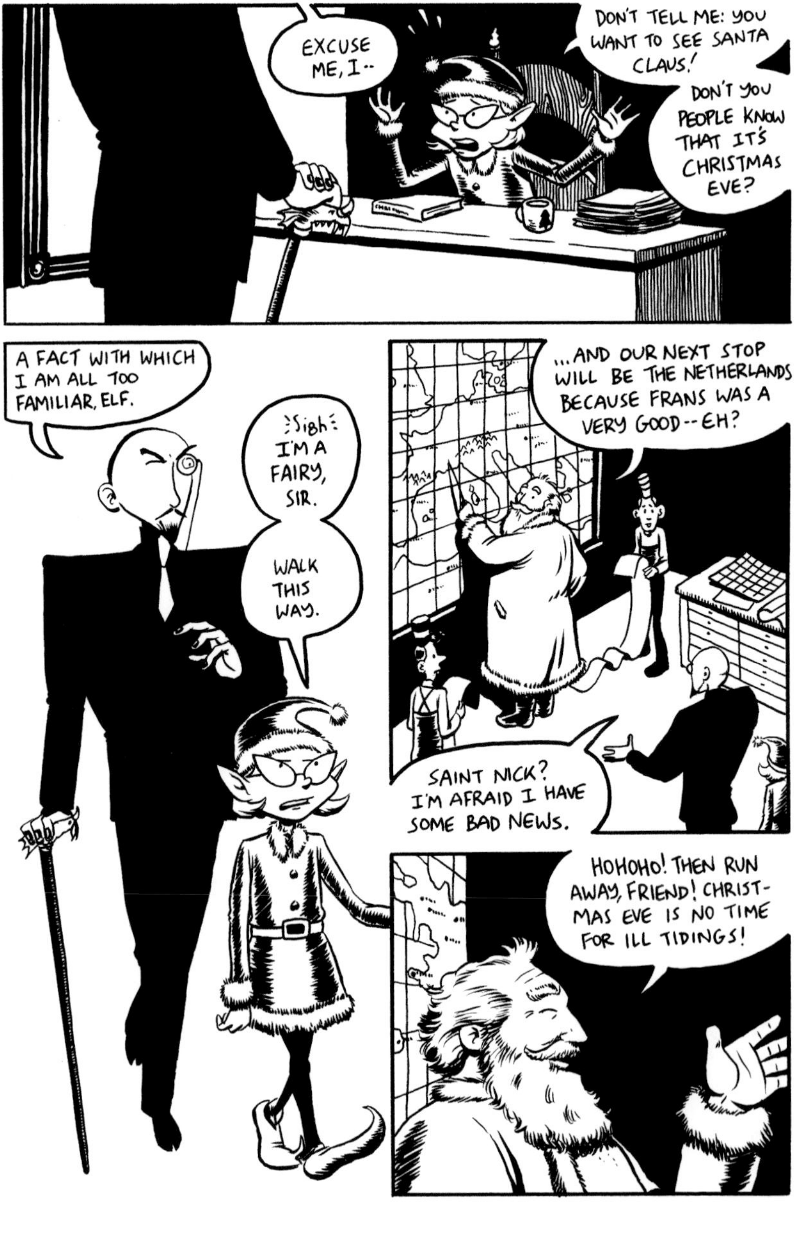
EXCUSE ME, I--
DON'T TELL ME: YOU WANT TO SEE SANTA CLAUS!
DON'T YOU PEOPLE KNOW THAT IT'S CHRISTMAS EVE?
A FACT WITH WHICH I AM ALL TOO FAMILIAR, ELF.
Sigh I'M A FAIRY, SIR.
WALK THIS WAY.
...AND OUR NEXT STOP WILL BE THE NETHERLANDS BECAUSE FRANS WAS A VERY GOOD--EH?
SAINT NICK? I'M AFRAID I HAVE SOME BAD NEWS.
HOHOHO! THEN RUN AWAY, FRIEND! CHRIST-MAS EVE IS NO TIME FOR ILL TIDINGS!

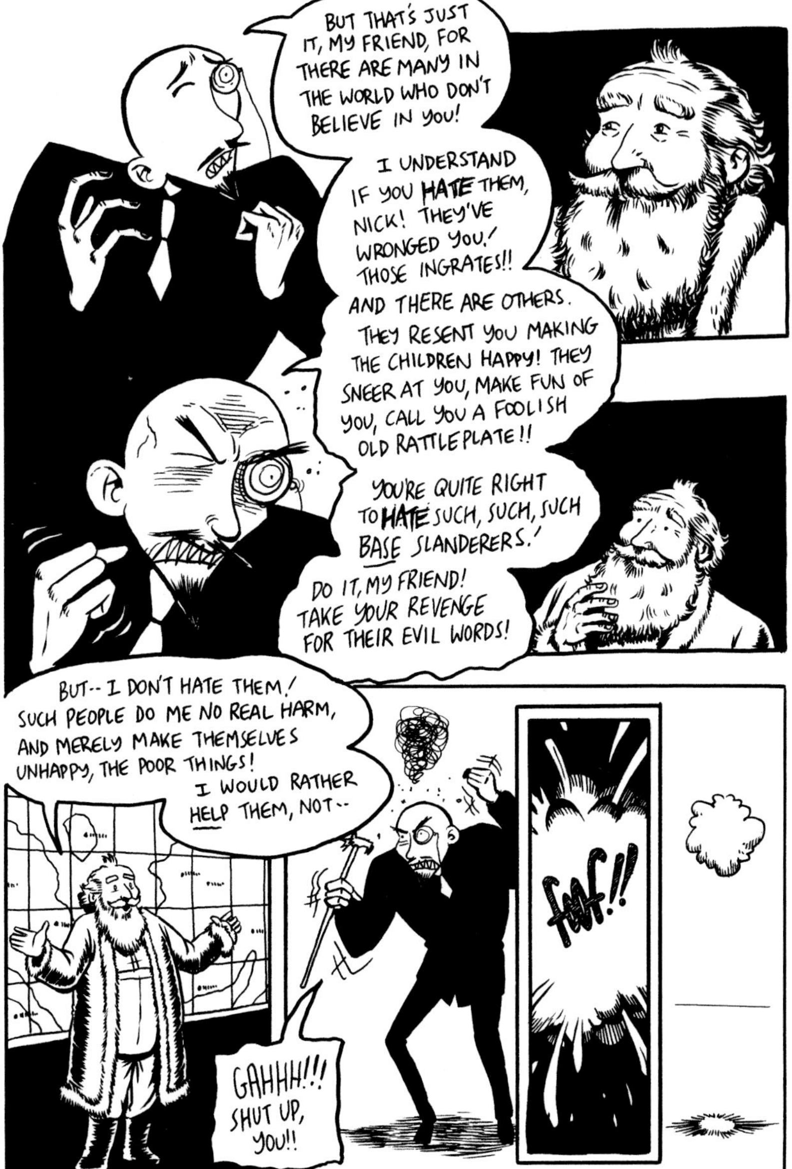
BUT THAT'S JUST IT, MY FRIEND, FOR THERE ARE MANY IN THE WORLD WHO DON'T BELIEVE IN YOU!
I UNDERSTAND IF YOU HATE THEM, NICK! THEY'VE WRONGED YOU! THOSE INGRATES!!
AND THERE ARE OTHERS.
THEY RESENT YOU MAKING THE CHILDREN HAPPY! THEY SNEER AT YOU, MAKE FUN OF YOU, CALL YOU A FOOLISH OLD RATTLEPLATE!!
YOU'RE QUITE RIGHT TO HATE SUCH, SUCH, SUCH BASE SLANDERERS!
DO IT, MY FRIEND! TAKE YOUR REVENGE FOR THEIR EVIL WORDS!
BUT-- I DON'T HATE THEM! SUCH PEOPLE DO ME NO REAL HARM, AND MERELY MAKE THEMSELVES UNHAPPY, THE POOR THINGS!
I WOULD RATHER HELP THEM, NOT--
GAHHH!!! SHUT UP, YOU!!
FOOF!!

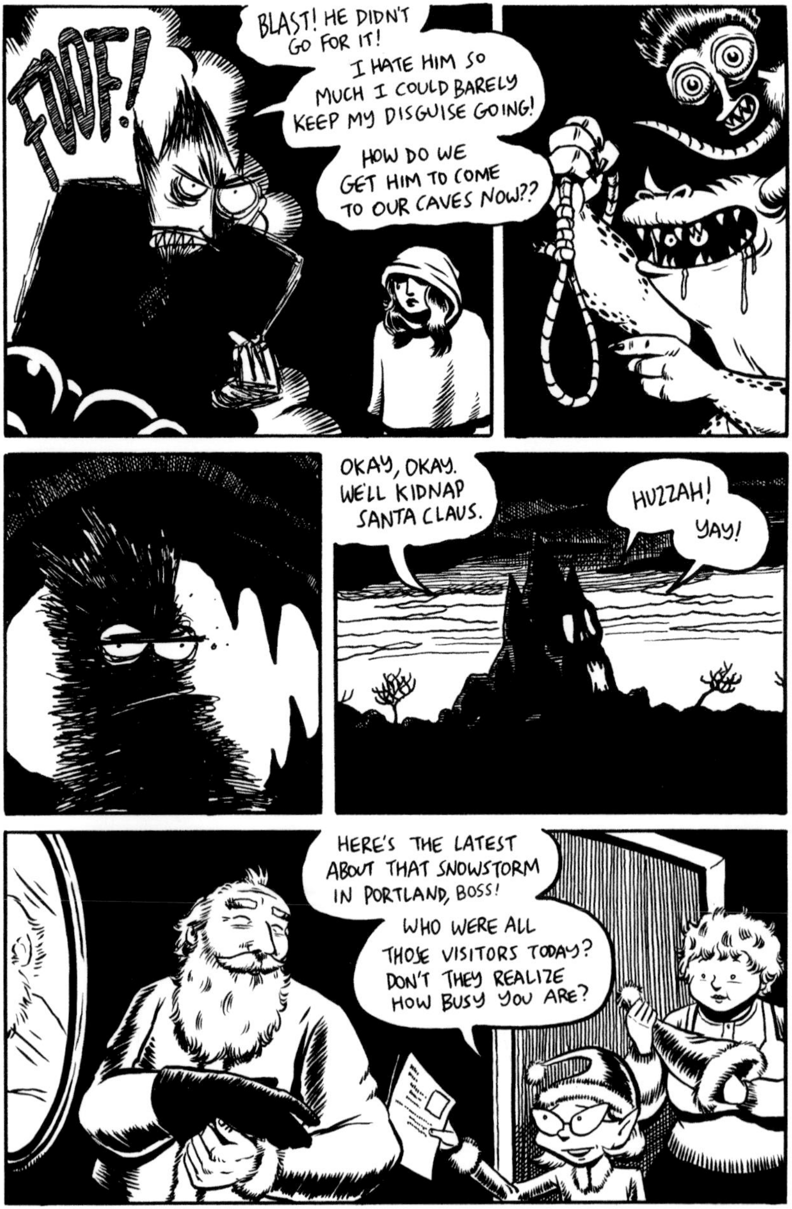
FOOF!
BLAST! HE DIDN'T GO FOR IT!
I HATE HIM SO MUCH I COULD BARELY KEEP MY DISGUISE GOING!
HOW DO WE GET HIM TO COME TO OUR CAVES NOW??
OKAY, OKAY. WE'LL KIDNAP SANTA CLAUS.
HUZZAH!
YAY!
HERE'S THE LATEST ABOUT THAT SNOWSTORM IN PORTLAND, BOSS!
WHO WERE ALL THOSE VISITORS TODAY? DON'T THEY REALIZE HOW BUSY YOU ARE?

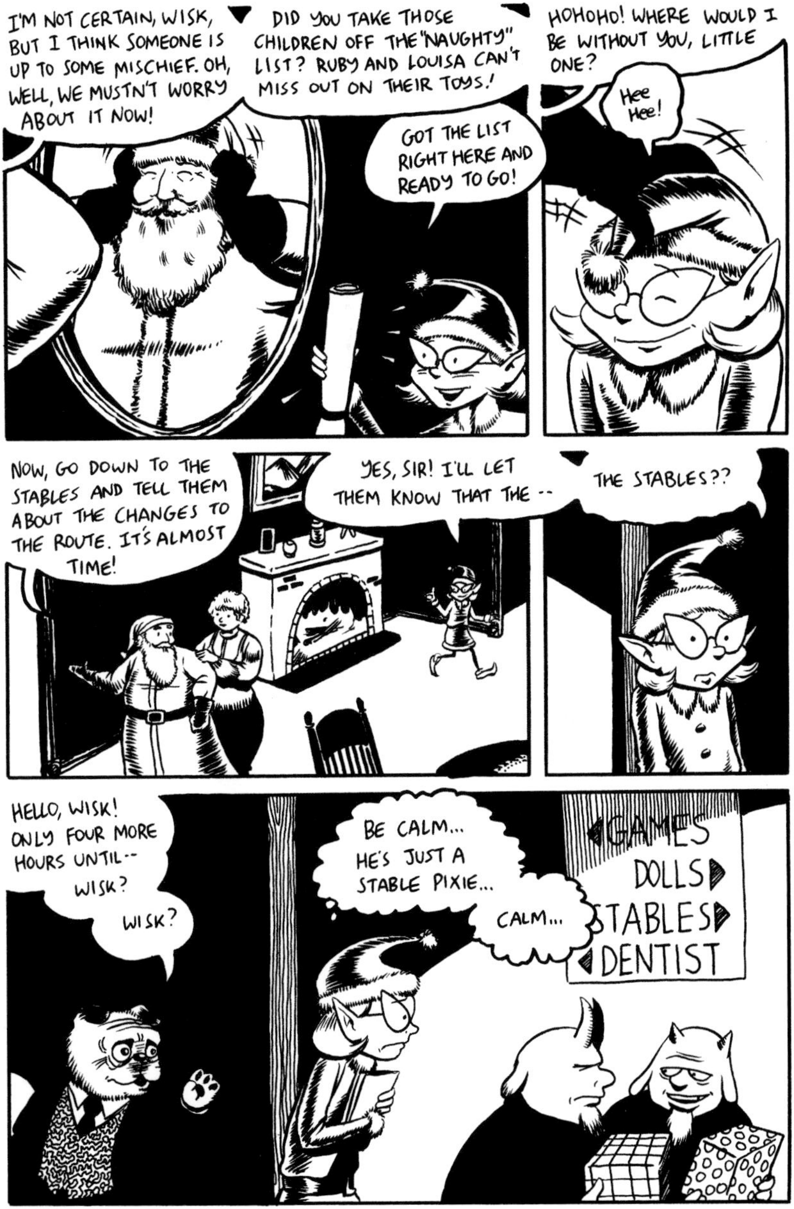
I'M NOT CERTAIN, WISK, BUT I THINK SOMEONE IS UP TO SOME MISCHIEF. OH, WELL, WE MUSTN'T WORRY ABOUT IT NOW!
DID YOU TAKE THOSE CHILDREN OFF THE "NAUGHTY" LIST? RUBY AND LOUISA CAN'T MISS OUT ON THEIR TOYS!
GOT THE LIST RIGHT HERE AND READY TO GO!
HOHOHO! WHERE WOULD I BE WITHOUT YOU, LITTLE ONE?
Hee Hee!
NOW, GO DOWN TO THE STABLES AND TELL THEM ABOUT THE CHANGES TO THE ROUTE. IT'S ALMOST TIME!
YES, SIR! I'LL LET THEM KNOW THAT THE --
THE STABLES??
HELLO, WISK! ONLY FOUR MORE HOURS UNTIL--
WISK?
WISK?
BE CALM... HE'S JUST A STABLE PIXIE...
CALM...
GAMES
DOLLS
STABLES
DENTIST

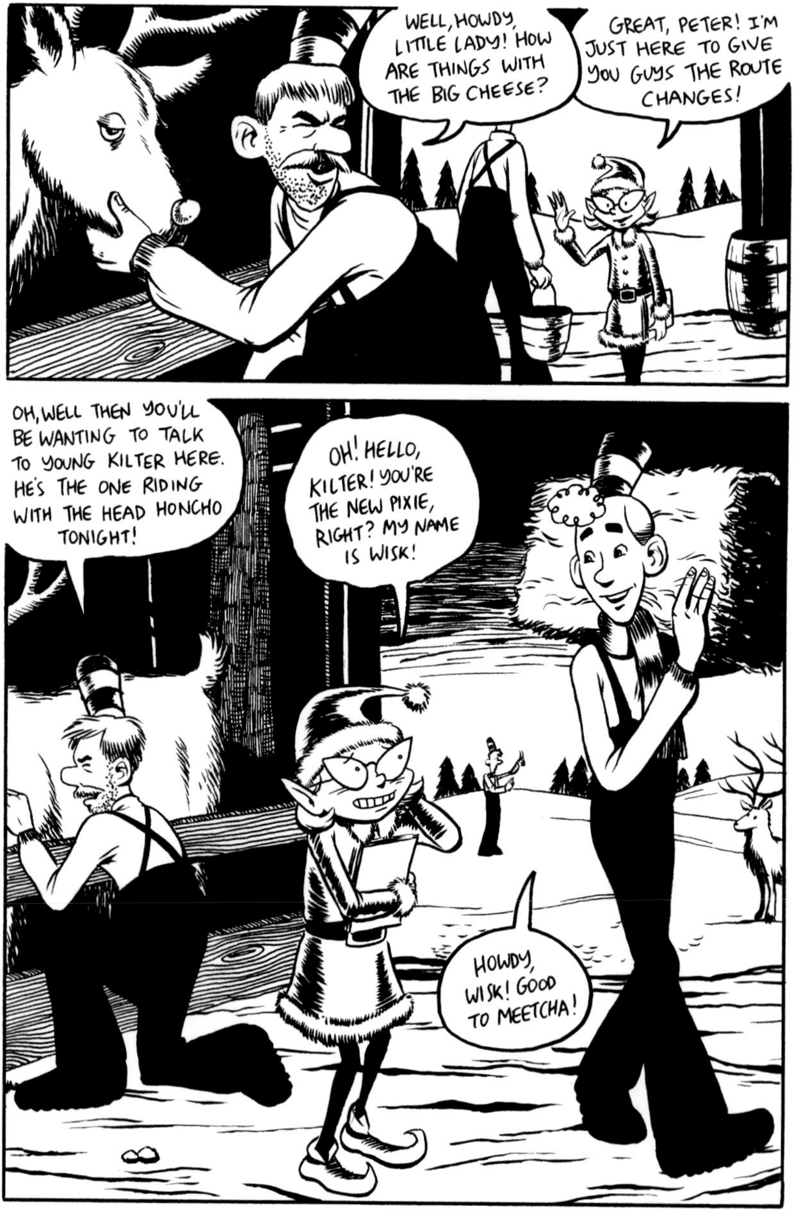
WELL, HOWDY, LITTLE LADY! HOW ARE THINGS WITH THE BIG CHEESE?
GREAT, PETER! I'M JUST HERE TO GIVE YOU GUYS THE ROUTE CHANGES!
OH, WELL THEN YOU'LL BE WANTING TO TALK TO YOUNG KILTER HERE. HE'S THE ONE RIDING WITH THE HEAD HONCHO TONIGHT!
OH! HELLO, KILTER! YOU'RE THE NEW PIXIE, RIGHT? MY NAME IS WISK!
HOWDY, WISK! GOOD TO MEETCHA!

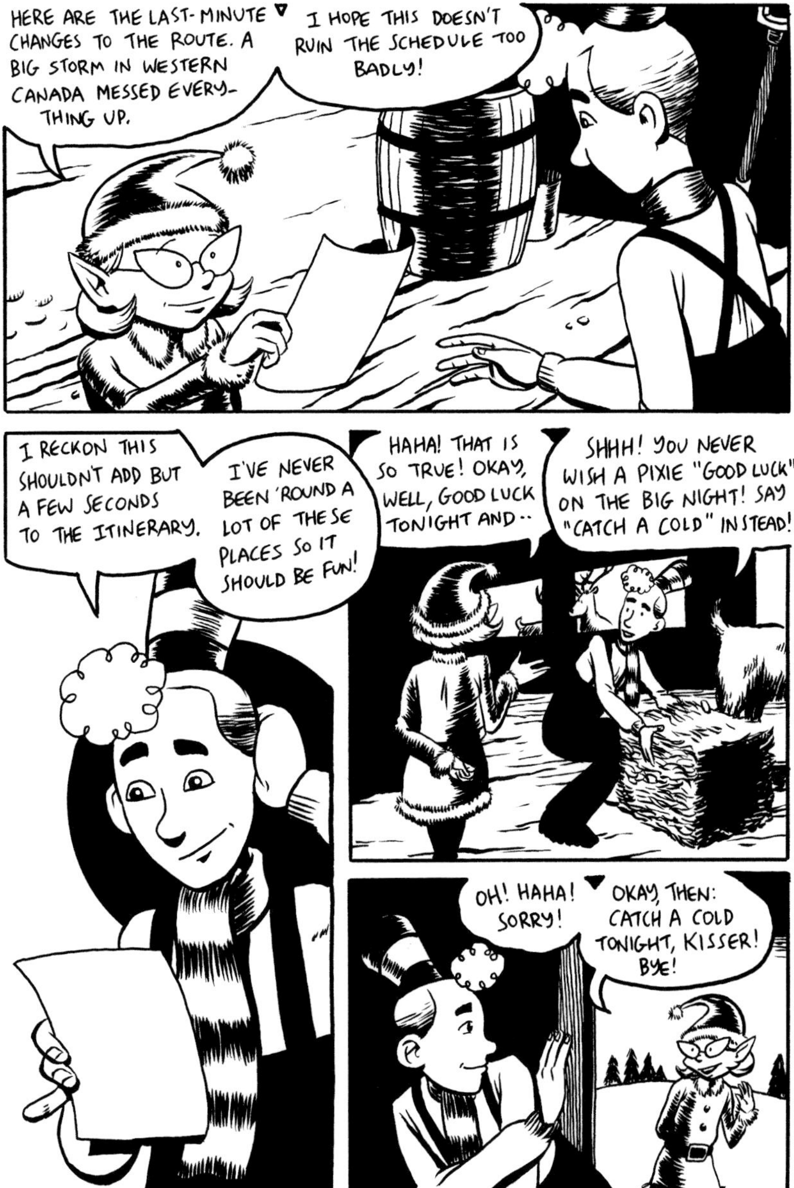
HERE ARE THE LAST-MINUTE CHANGES TO THE ROUTE. A BIG STORM IN WESTERN CANADA MESSED EVERYTHING UP.
I HOPE THIS DOESN'T RUIN THE SCHEDULE TOO BADLY!
I RECKON THIS SHOULDN'T ADD BUT A FEW SECONDS TO THE ITINERARY.
I'VE NEVER BEEN 'ROUND A LOT OF THESE PLACES SO IT SHOULD BE FUN!
HAHA! THAT IS SO TRUE! OKAY, WELL, GOOD LUCK TONIGHT AND..
SHHH! YOU NEVER WISH A PIXIE "GOOD LUCK" ON THE BIG NIGHT! SAY "CATCH A COLD" INSTEAD!
OH! HAHA! SORRY!
OKAY, THEN: CATCH A COLD TONIGHT, KISSER! BYE!

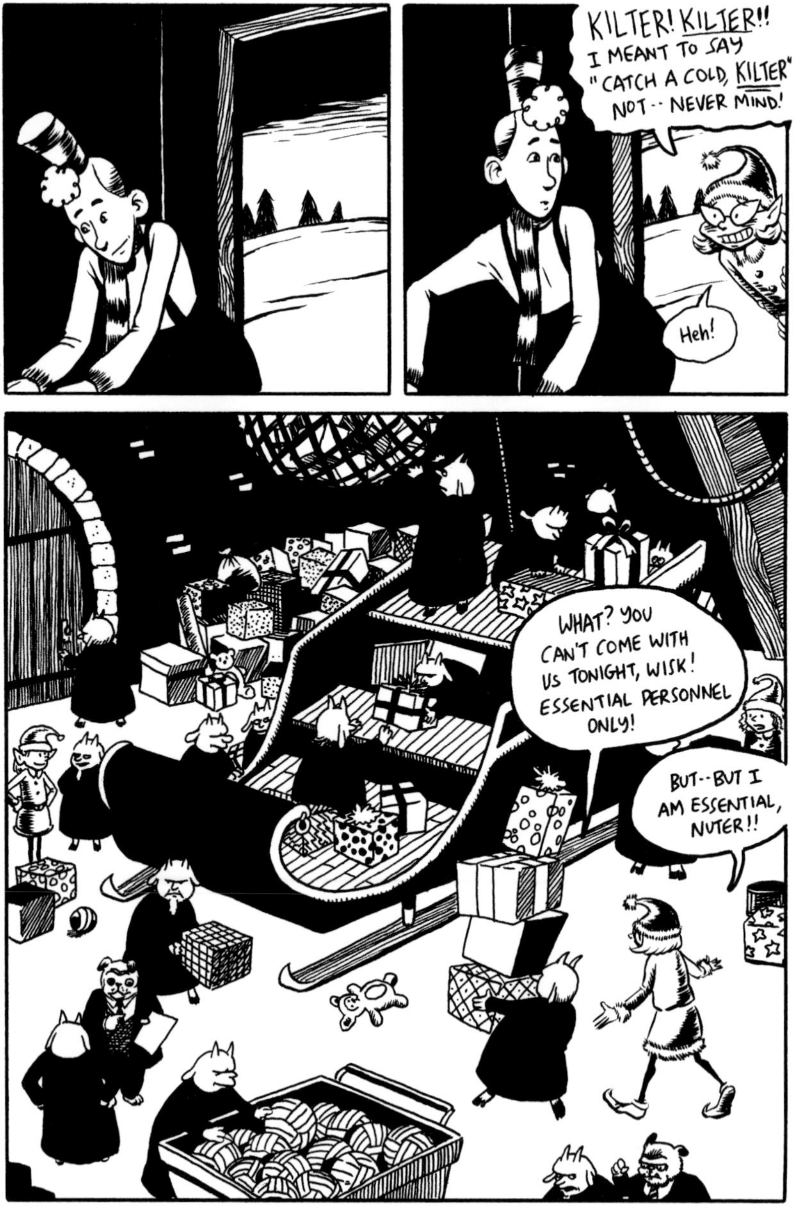

KILTER! KILTER!! I MEANT TO SAY "CATCH A COLD, KILTER" NOT-- NEVER MIND!
Heh!
WHAT? YOU CAN'T COME WITH US TONIGHT, WISK! ESSENTIAL PERSONNEL ONLY!
BUT--BUT I AM ESSENTIAL, NUTER!!

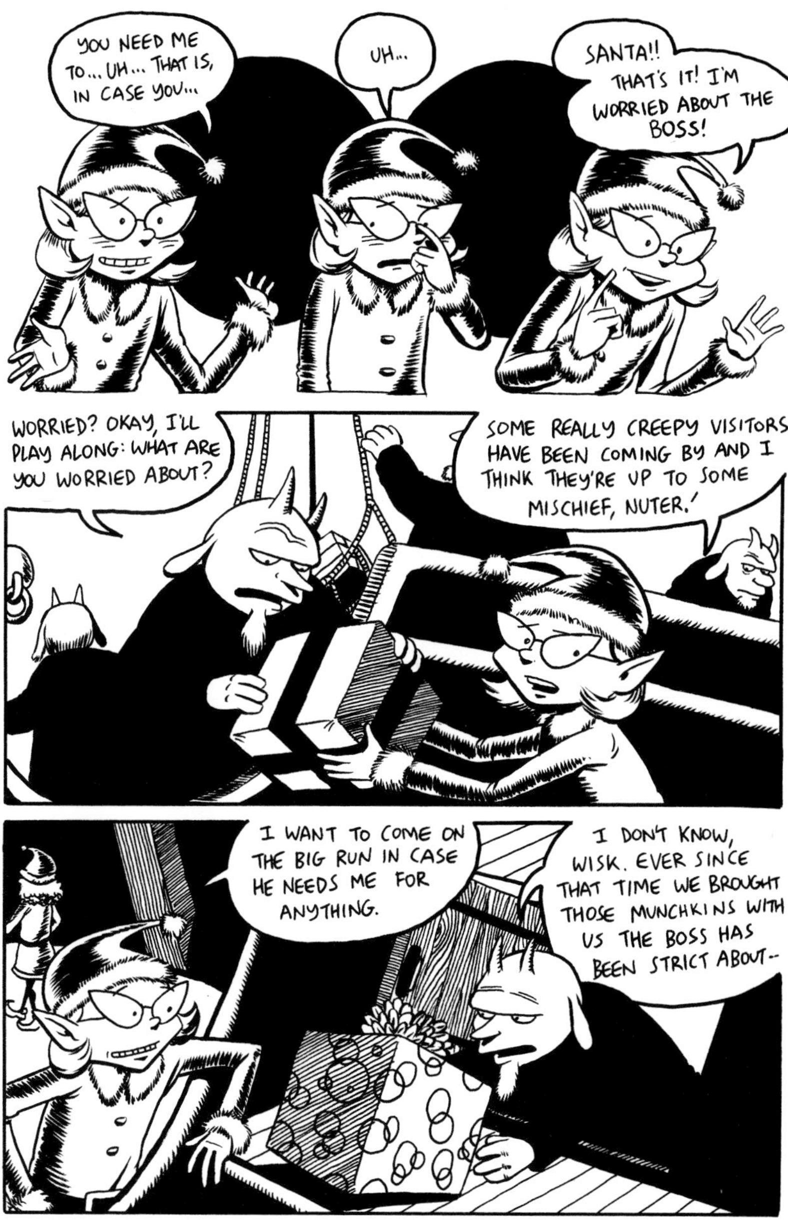
YOU NEED ME TO... UH... THAT IS, IN CASE YOU...
UH...
SANTA!! THAT'S IT! I'M WORRIED ABOUT THE BOSS!
WORRIED? OKAY, I'LL PLAY ALONG: WHAT ARE YOU WORRIED ABOUT?
SOME REALLY CREEPY VISITORS HAVE BEEN COMING BY AND I THINK THEY'RE UP TO SOME MISCHIEF, NUTER.
I WANT TO COME ON THE BIG RUN IN CASE HE NEEDS ME FOR ANYTHING.
I DON'T KNOW, WISK. EVER SINCE THAT TIME WE BROUGHT THOSE MUNCHKINS WITH US THE BOSS HAS BEEN STRICT ABOUT--

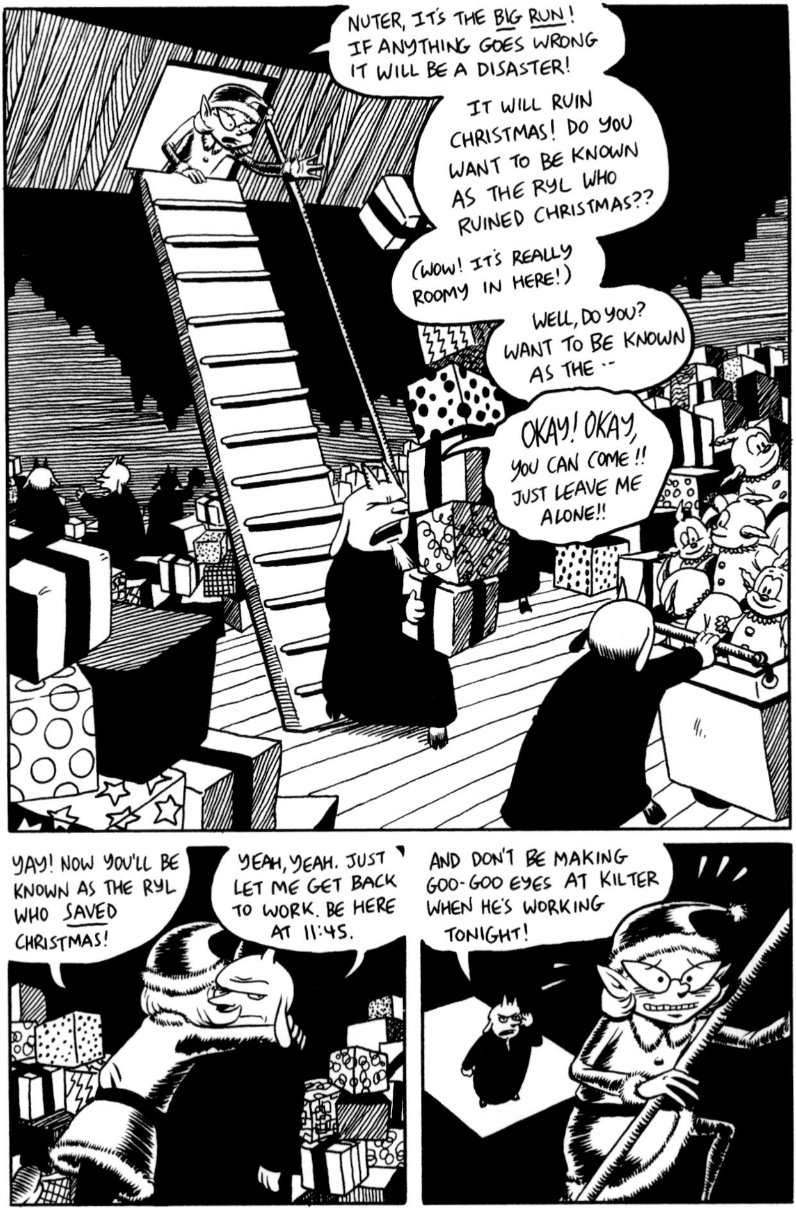
NUTER, IT'S THE BIG RUN! IF ANYTHING GOES WRONG IT WILL BE A DISASTER!
IT WILL RUIN CHRISTMAS! DO YOU WANT TO BE KNOWN AS THE RYL WHO RUINED CHRISTMAS??
(WOW! IT'S REALLY ROOMY IN HERE!)
WELL, DO YOU? WANT TO BE KNOWN AS THE --
OKAY! OKAY, YOU CAN COME!! JUST LEAVE ME ALONE!!
YAY! NOW YOU'LL BE KNOWN AS THE RYL WHO SAVED CHRISTMAS!
YEAH, YEAH. JUST LET ME GET BACK TO WORK. BE HERE AT 11:45.
AND DON'T BE MAKING GOO-GOO EYES AT KILTER WHEN HE'S WORKING TONIGHT!

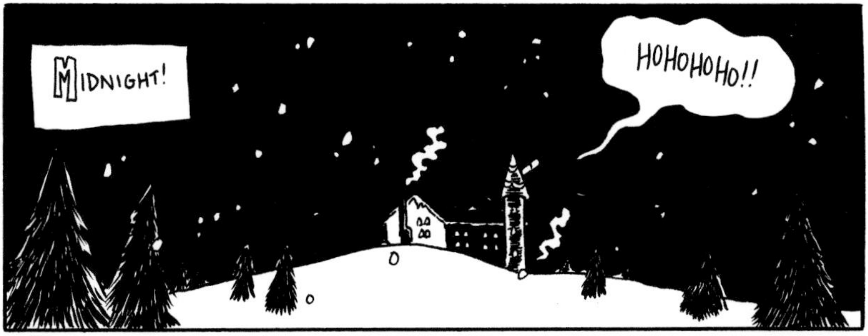
MIDNIGHT!
HOHOHOHOHO!!

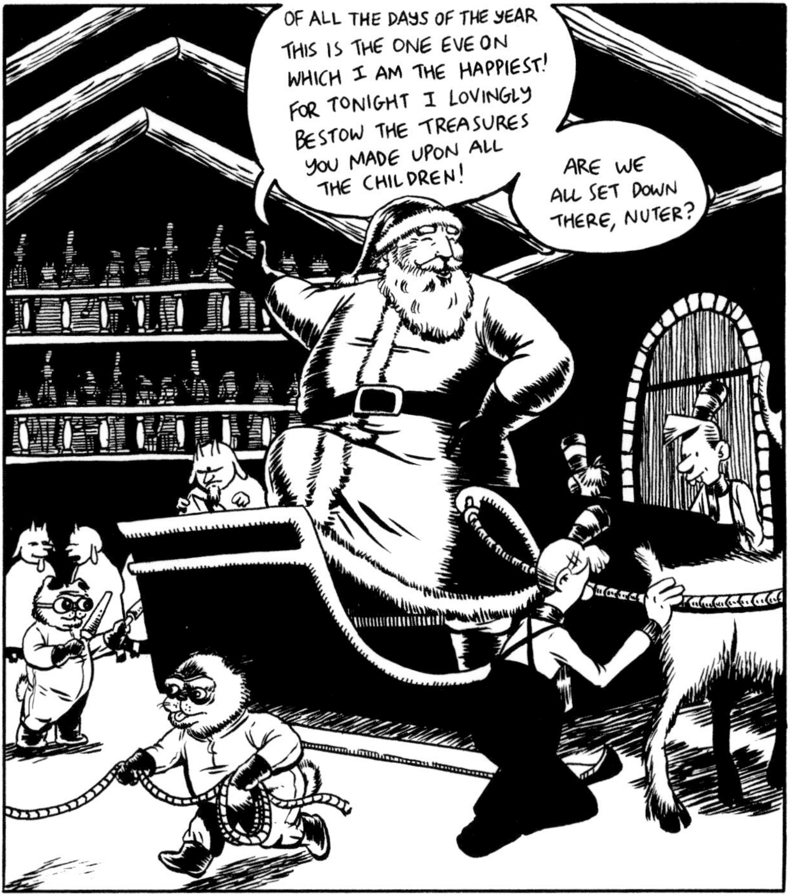
OF ALL THE DAYS OF THE YEAR THIS IS THE ONE EVE ON WHICH I AM THE HAPPIEST! FOR TONIGHT I LOVINGLY BESTOW THE TREASURES YOU MADE UPON ALL THE CHILDREN!
ARE WE ALL SET DOWN THERE, NUTER?

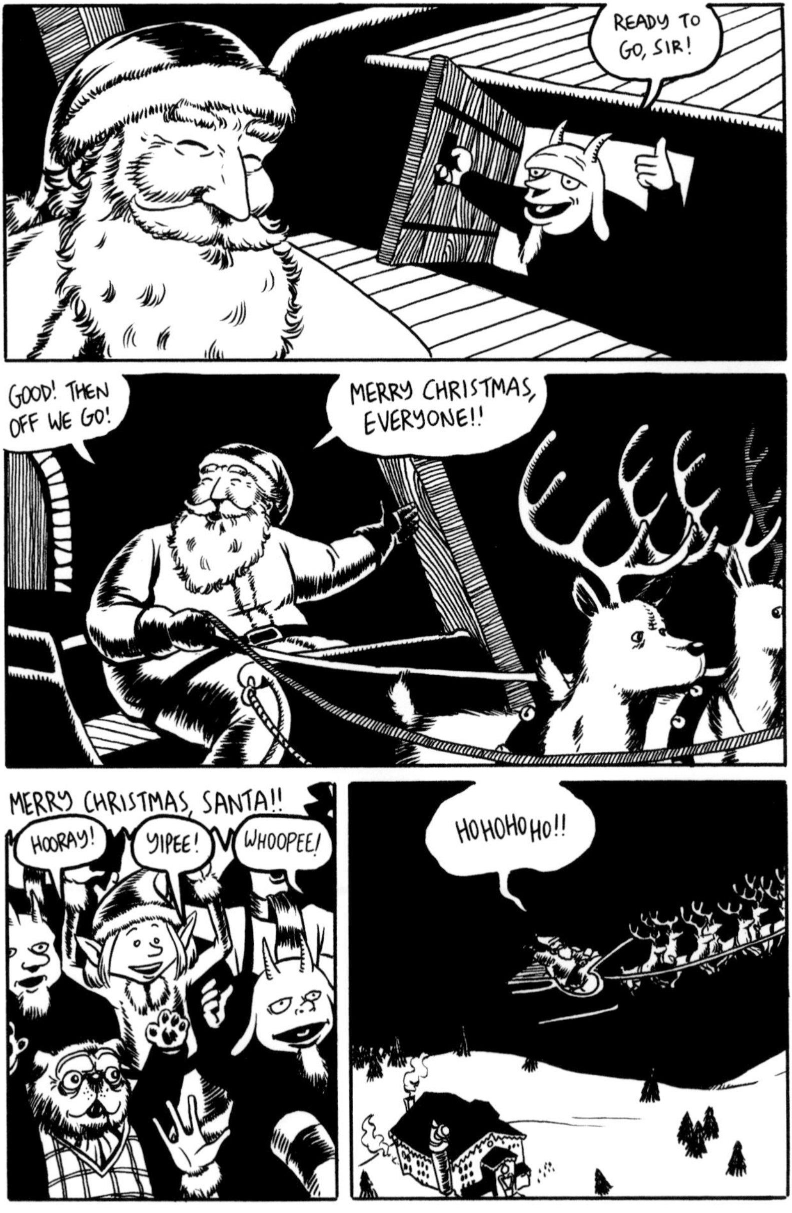
READY TO GO, SIR!
GOOD! THEN OFF WE GO!
MERRY CHRISTMAS, EVERYONE!!
MERRY CHRISTMAS, SANTA!!
HOORAY!
YIPEE!
WHOOPEE!
HOHOHOHOHO!!

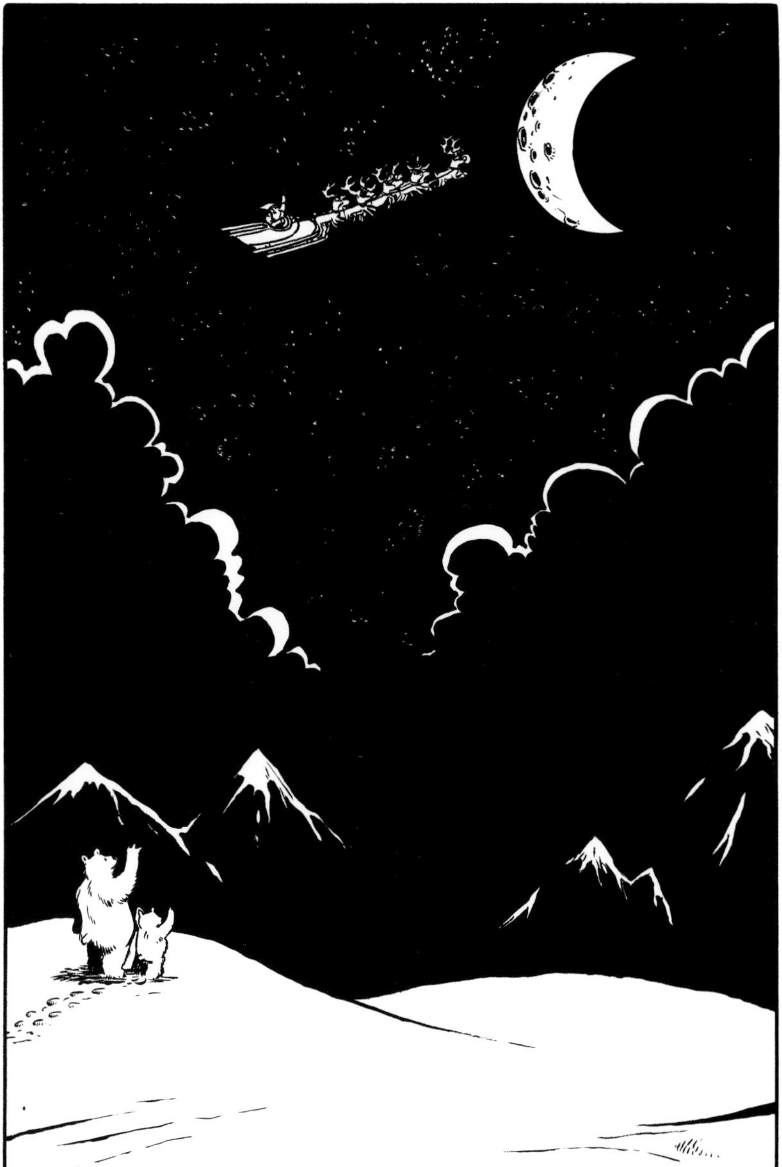

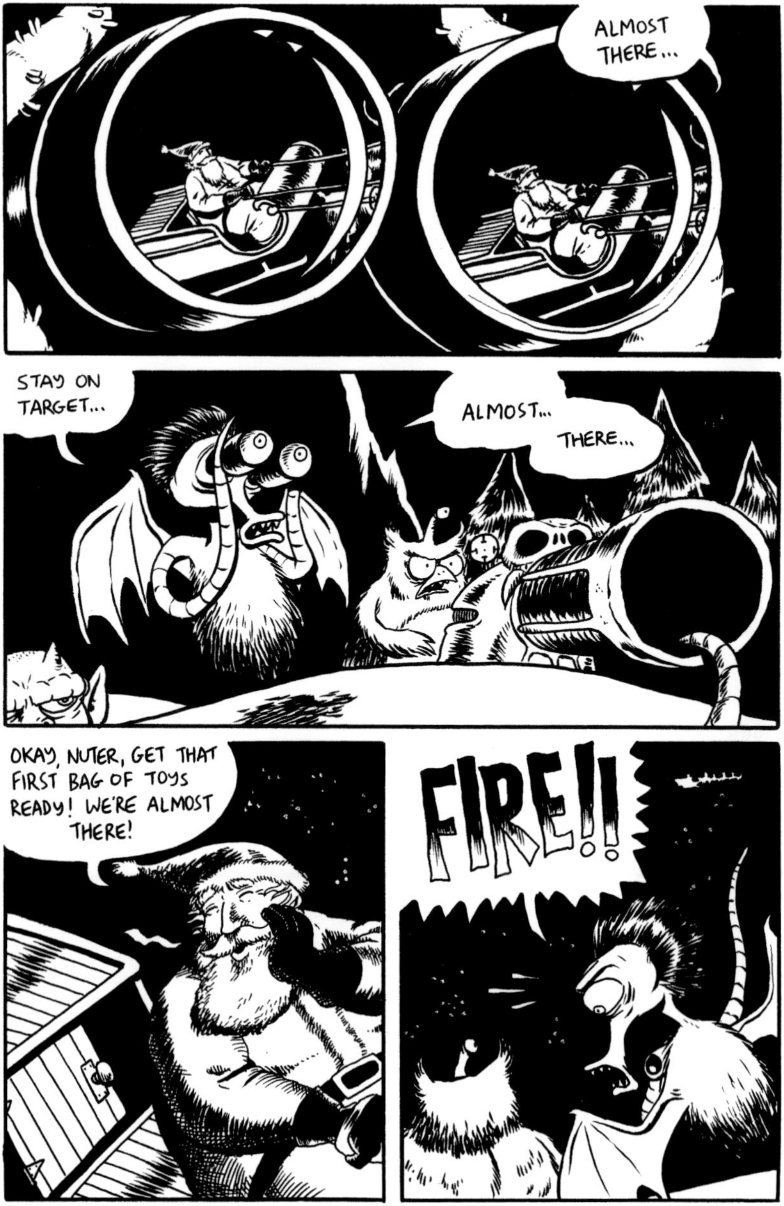
ALMOST THERE...
STAY ON TARGET...
ALMOST... THERE...
OKAY, NUTER, GET THAT FIRST BAG OF TOYS READY! WE'RE ALMOST THERE!
FIRE!!

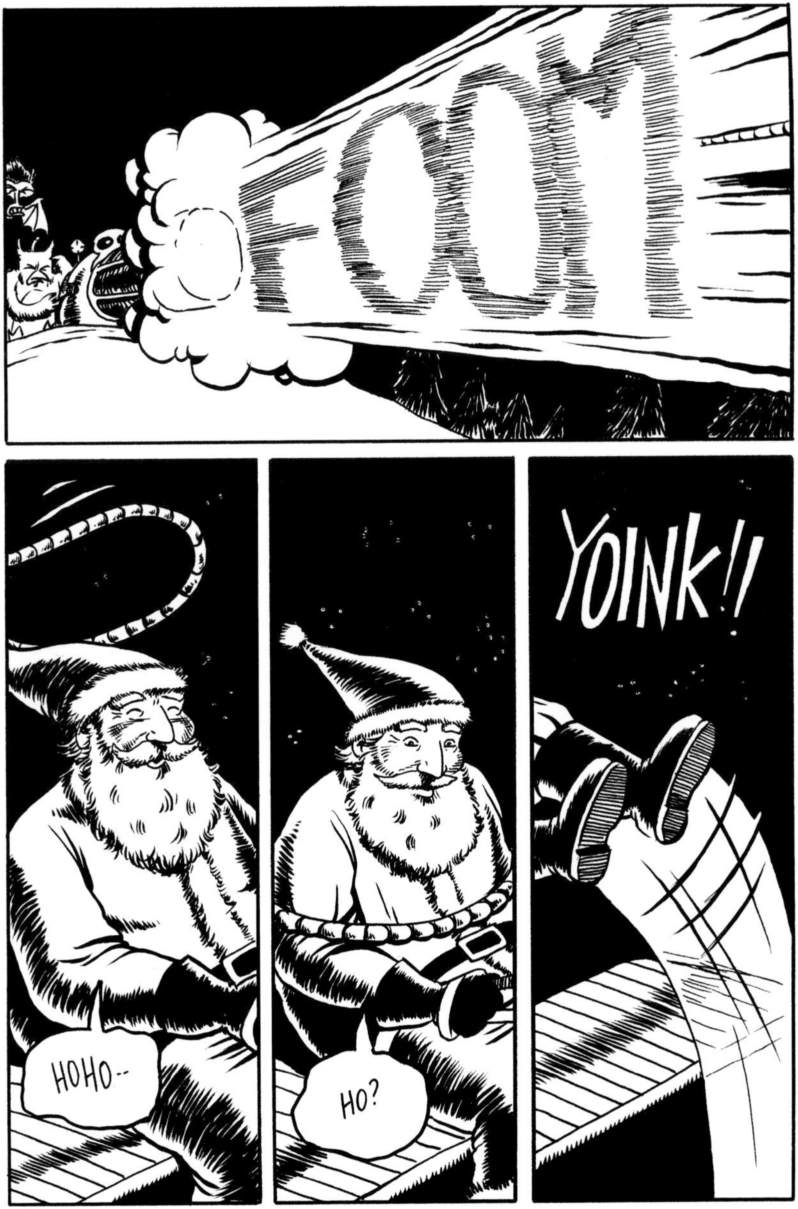
FOOM
HOHO--
HO?
YOINK!!

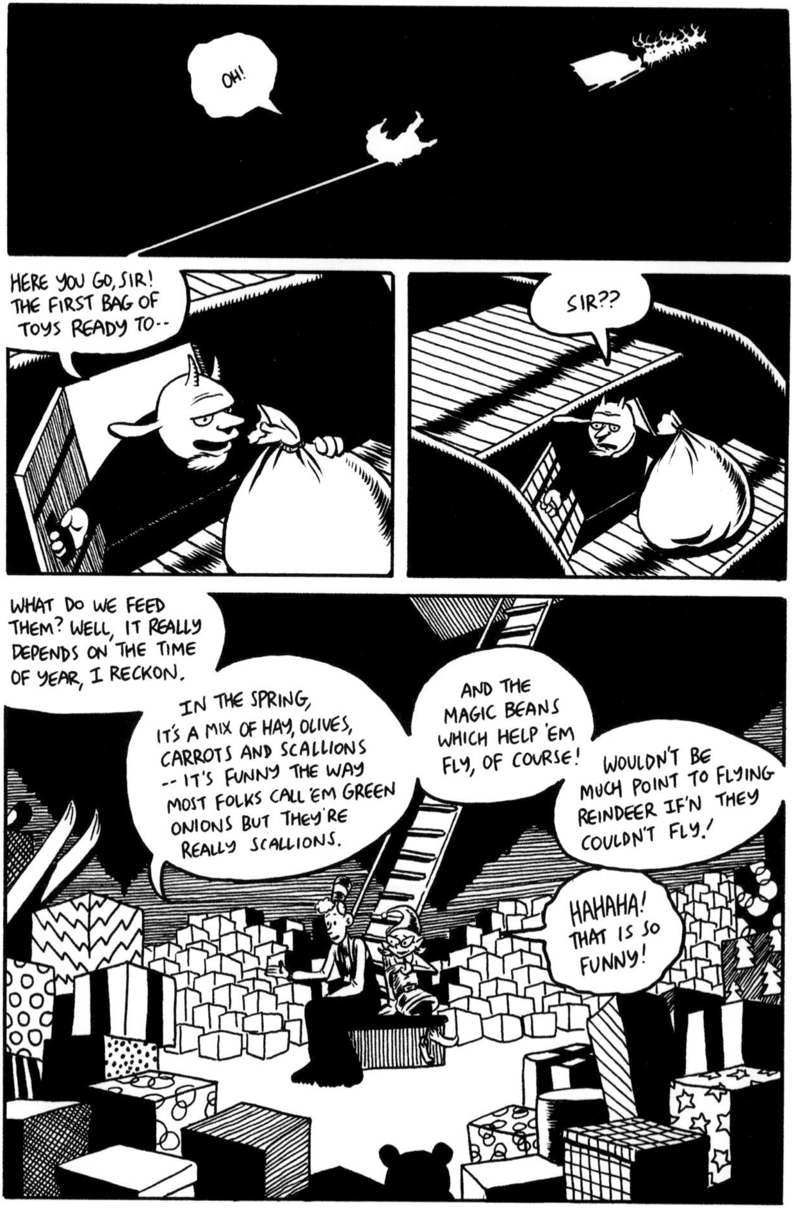
OH!
HERE YOU GO, SIR! THE FIRST BAG OF TOYS READY TO--
SIR??
WHAT DO WE FEED THEM? WELL, IT REALLY DEPENDS ON THE TIME OF YEAR, I RECKON.
IN THE SPRING, IT'S A MIX OF HAY, OLIVES, CARROTS AND SCALLIONS -- IT'S FUNNY THE WAY MOST FOLKS CALL 'EM GREEN ONIONS BUT THEY'RE REALLY SCALLIONS.
AND THE MAGIC BEANS WHICH HELP 'EM FLY, OF COURSE!
WOULDN'T BE MUCH POINT TO FLYING REINDEER IF'N THEY COULDN'T FLY!
HAHAHA! THAT IS SO FUNNY!

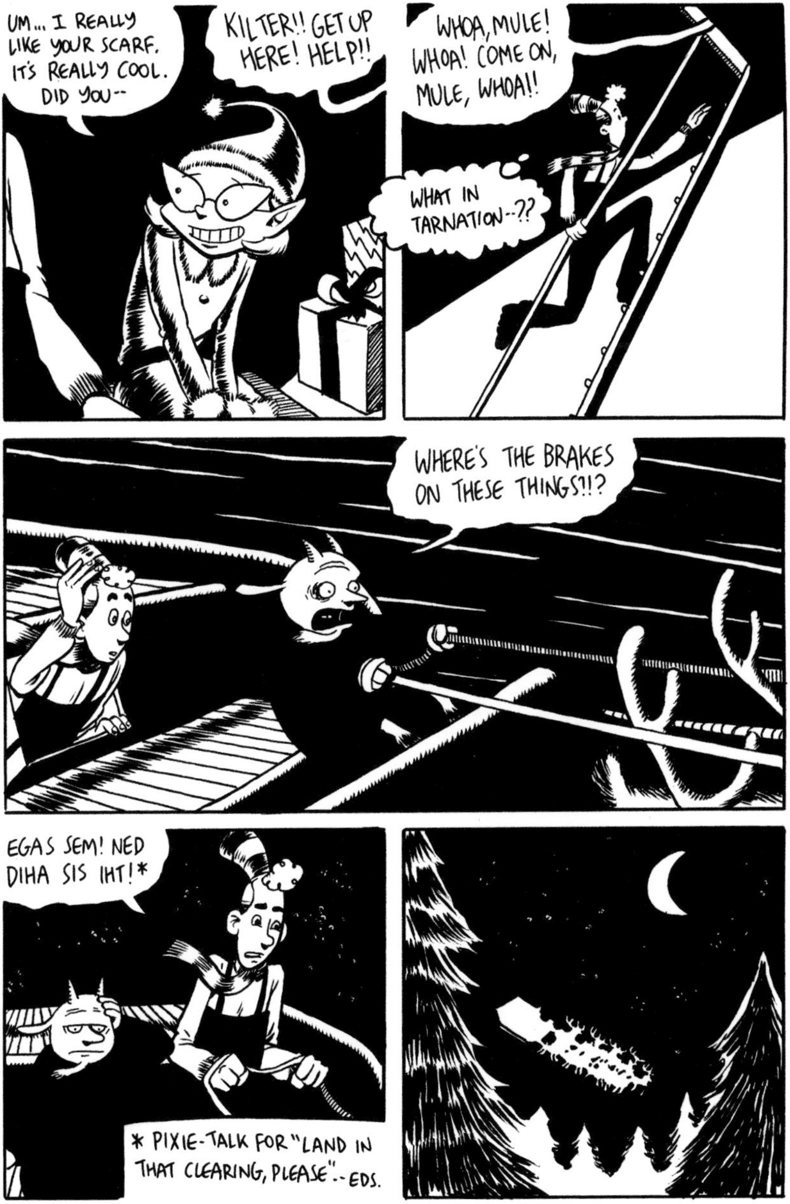
UM... I REALLY LIKE YOUR SCARF. IT'S REALLY COOL. DID YOU--
KILTER!! GET UP HERE! HELP!!
WHOA, MULE! WHOA! COME ON, MULE, WHOA!!
WHAT IN TARNATION--??
WHERE'S THE BRAKES ON THESE THINGS?!!?
EGAS SEM! NED DIHA SIS IHT!*
* PIXIE-TALK FOR "LAND IN THAT CLEARING, PLEASE".-- EDS.

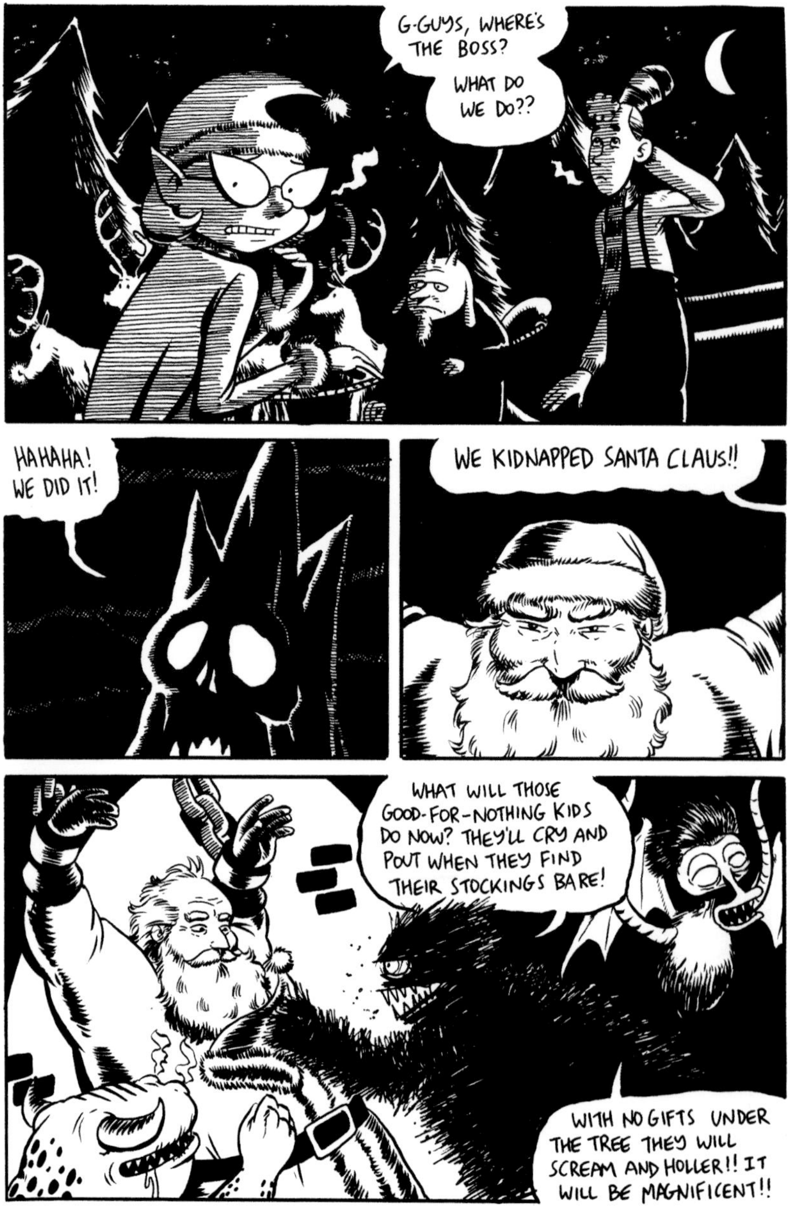
G-GUYS, WHERE'S THE BOSS?
WHAT DO WE DO??
HAHAHA! WE DID IT!
WE KIDNAPPED SANTA CLAUS!!
WHAT WILL THOSE GOOD-FOR-NOTHING KIDS DO NOW? THEY'LL CRY AND POUT WHEN THEY FIND THEIR STOCKINGS BARE!
WITH NO GIFTS UNDER THE TREE THEY WILL SCREAM AND HOLLER!! IT WILL BE MAGNIFICENT!!

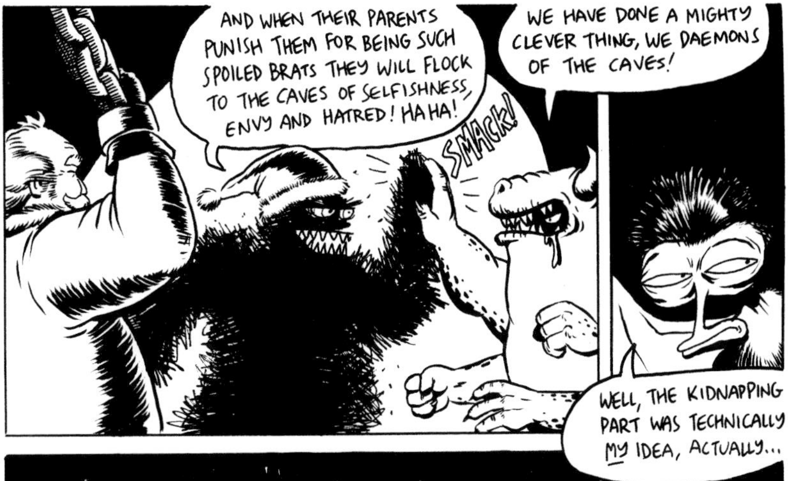
AND WHEN THEIR PARENTS PUNISH THEM FOR BEING SUCH SPOILED BRATS THEY WILL FLOCK TO THE CAVES OF SELFISHNESS, ENVY AND HATRED! HAHA!
SMACK!
WE HAVE DONE A MIGHTY CLEVER THING, WE DAEMONS OF THE CAVES!
WELL, THE KIDNAPPING PART WAS TECHNICALLY MY IDEA, ACTUALLY...

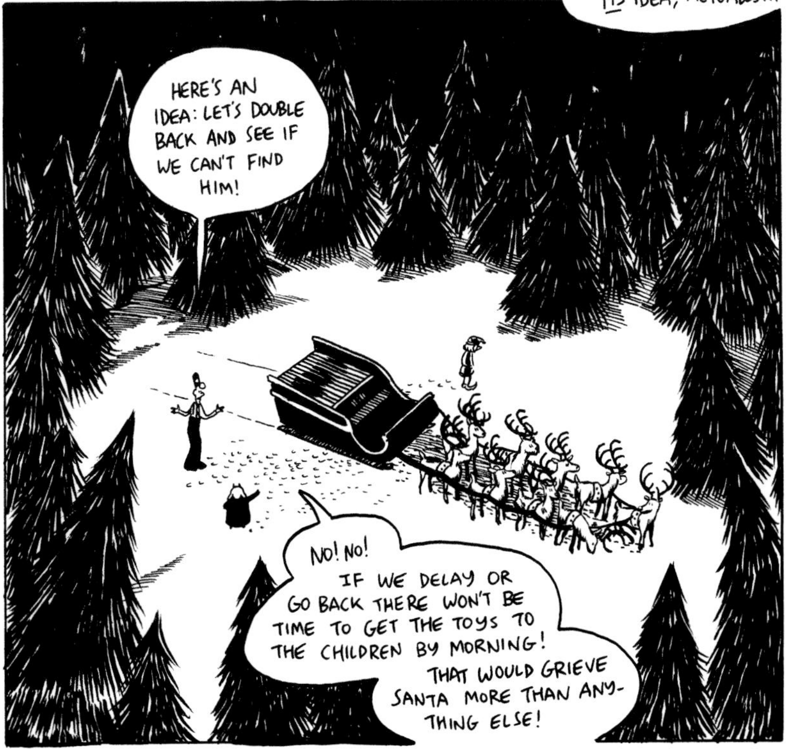
HERE'S AN IDEA: LET'S DOUBLE BACK AND SEE IF WE CAN'T FIND HIM!
NO! NO!
IF WE DELAY OR GO BACK THERE WON'T BE TIME TO GET THE TOYS TO THE CHILDREN BY MORNING!
THAT WOULD GRIEVE SANTA MORE THAN ANY-THING ELSE!

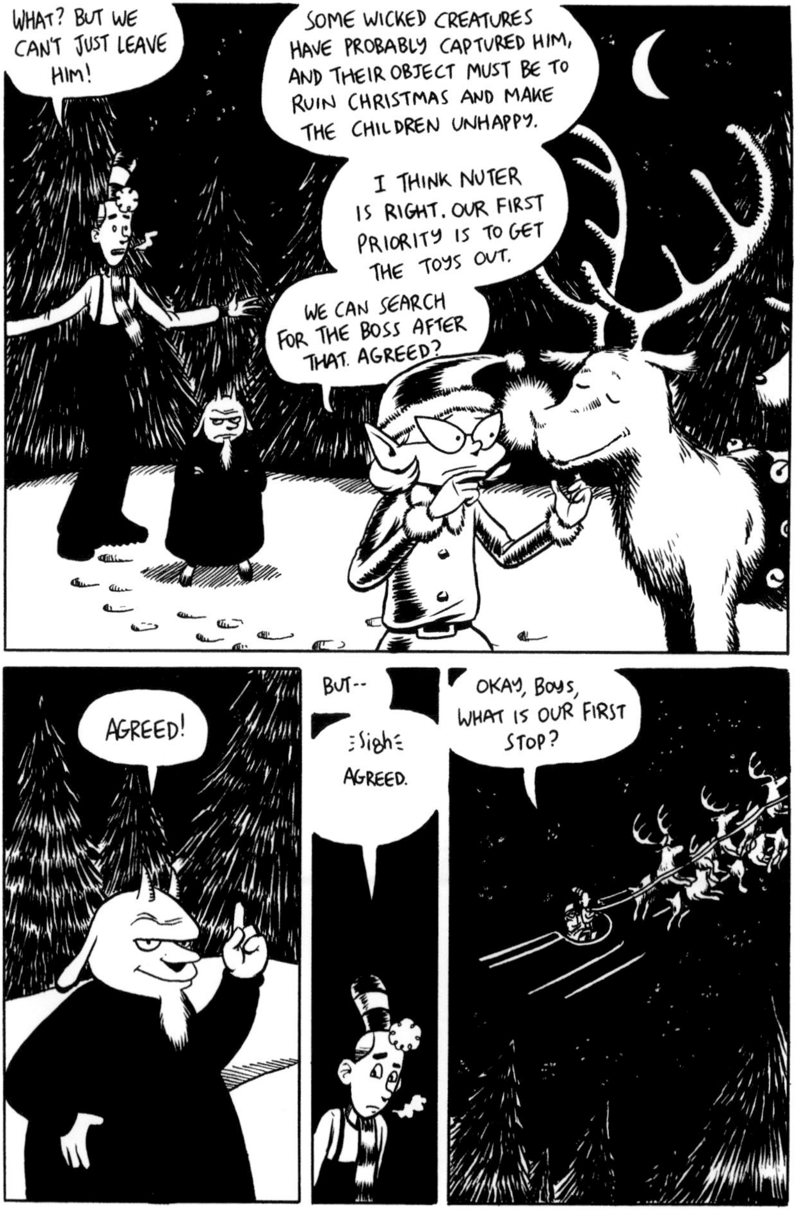
WHAT? BUT WE CAN'T JUST LEAVE HIM!
SOME WICKED CREATURES HAVE PROBABLY CAPTURED HIM, AND THEIR OBJECT MUST BE TO RUIN CHRISTMAS AND MAKE THE CHILDREN UNHAPPY.
I THINK NUTER IS RIGHT. OUR FIRST PRIORITY IS TO GET THE TOYS OUT.
WE CAN SEARCH FOR THE BOSS AFTER THAT. AGREED?
AGREED!
BUT--
Sigh
AGREED.
OKAY, BOYS, WHAT IS OUR FIRST STOP?

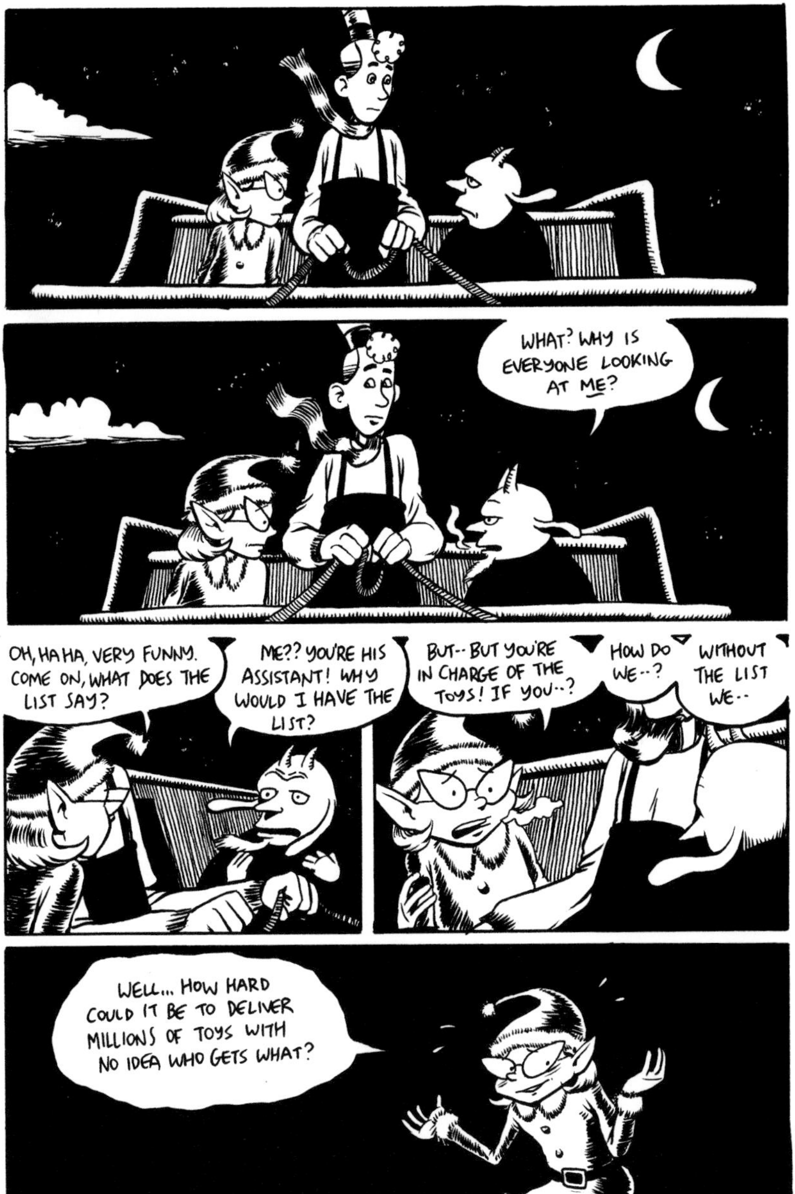
WHAT? WHY IS EVERYONE LOOKING AT ME?
OH, HA HA, VERY FUNNY. COME ON, WHAT DOES THE LIST SAY?
ME?? YOU'RE HIS ASSISTANT! WHY WOULD I HAVE THE LIST?
BUT-- BUT YOU'RE IN CHARGE OF THE TOYS! IF YOU--?
HOW DO WE--?
WITHOUT THE LIST WE--
WELL... HOW HARD COULD IT BE TO DELIVER MILLIONS OF TOYS WITH NO IDEA WHO GETS WHAT?

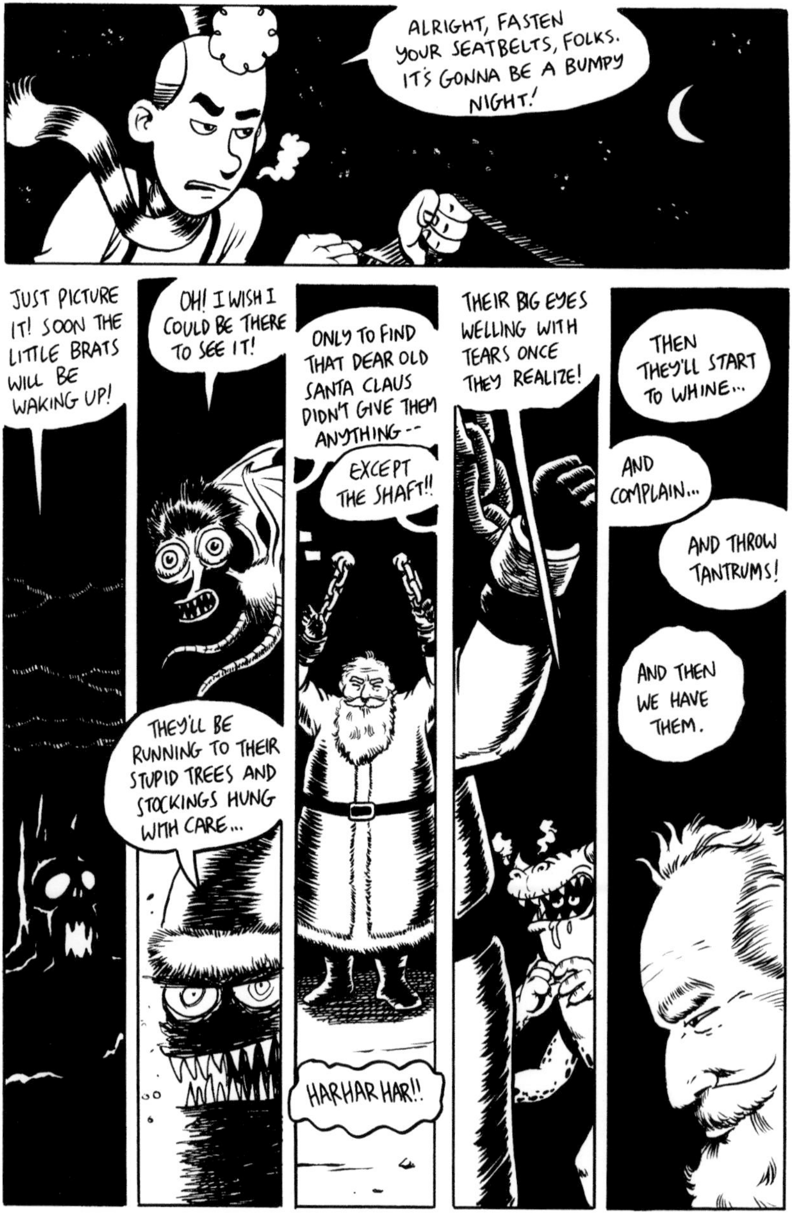
ALRIGHT, FASTEN YOUR SEATBELTS, FOLKS. IT'S GONNA BE A BUMPY NIGHT!
JUST PICTURE IT! SOON THE LITTLE BRATS WILL BE WAKING UP!
OH! I WISH I COULD BE THERE TO SEE IT!
THEY'LL BE RUNNING TO THEIR STUPID TREES AND STOCKINGS HUNG WITH CARE...
ONLY TO FIND THAT DEAR OLD SANTA CLAUS DIDN'T GIVE THEM ANYTHING--
EXCEPT THE SHAFT!!
HARHAR HAR!!
THEIR BIG EYES WELLING WITH TEARS ONCE THEY REALIZE!
THEN THEY'LL START TO WHINE...
AND COMPLAIN...
AND THROW TANTRUMS!
AND THEN WE HAVE THEM.

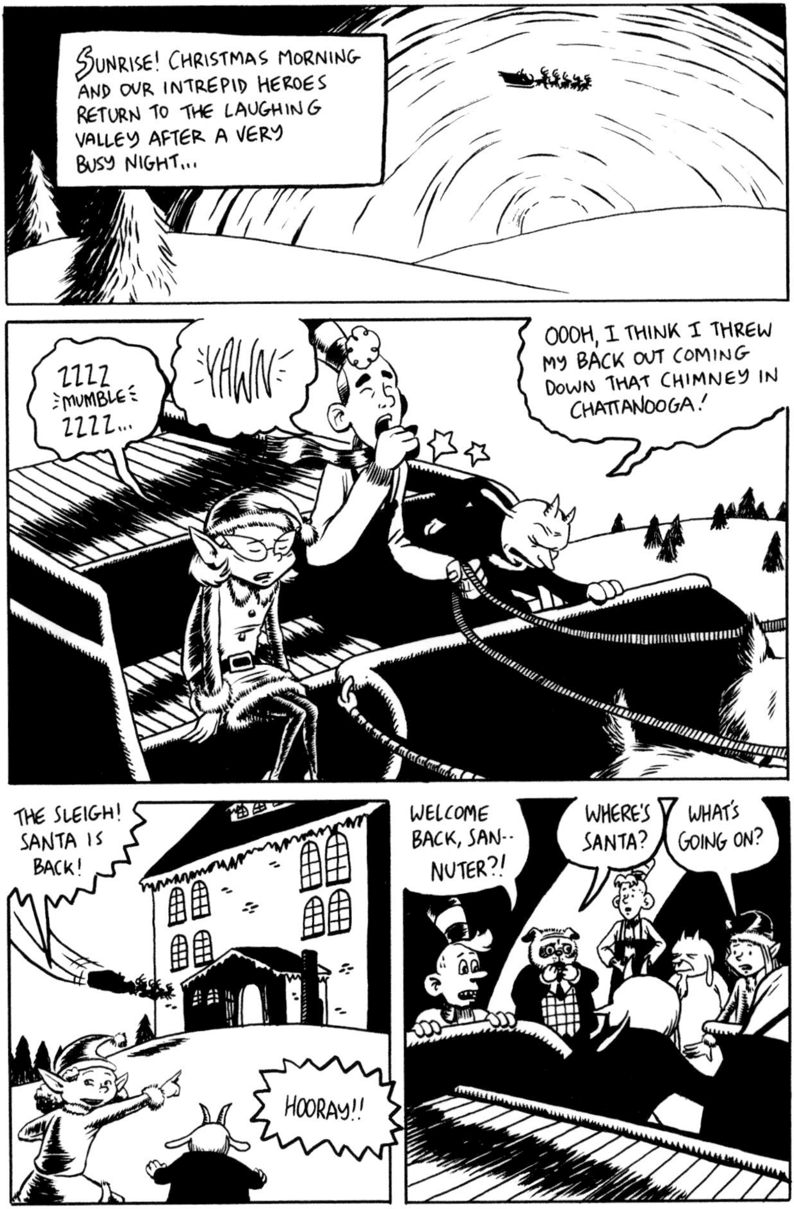
SUNRISE! CHRISTMAS MORNING AND OUR INTREPID HEROES RETURN TO THE LAUGHING VALLEY AFTER A VERY BUSY NIGHT...
ZZZZ MUMBLE ZZZZ...
YAWN
OOOH, I THINK I THREW MY BACK OUT COMING DOWN THAT CHIMNEY IN CHATTANOOGA!
THE SLEIGH! SANTA IS BACK!
HOORAY!!
WELCOME BACK, SAN-- NUTER?!
WHERE'S SANTA?
WHAT'S GOING ON?

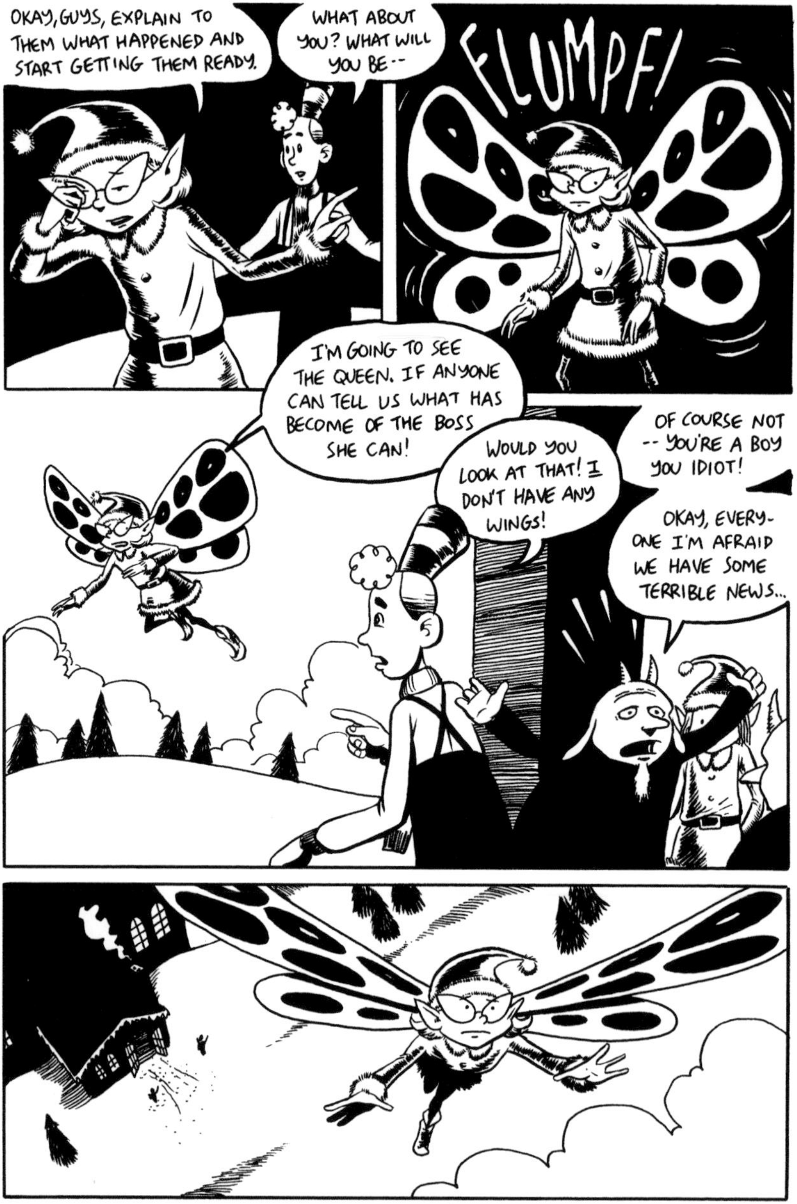
OKAY, GUYS, EXPLAIN TO THEM WHAT HAPPENED AND START GETTING THEM READY.
WHAT ABOUT YOU? WHAT WILL YOU BE--
FLUMPF!
I'M GOING TO SEE THE QUEEN. IF ANYONE CAN TELL US WHAT HAS BECOME OF THE BOSS SHE CAN!
WOULD YOU LOOK AT THAT! I DON'T HAVE ANY WINGS!
OF COURSE NOT -- YOU'RE A BOY YOU IDIOT!
OKAY, EVERYONE I'M AFRAID WE HAVE SOME TERRIBLE NEWS...

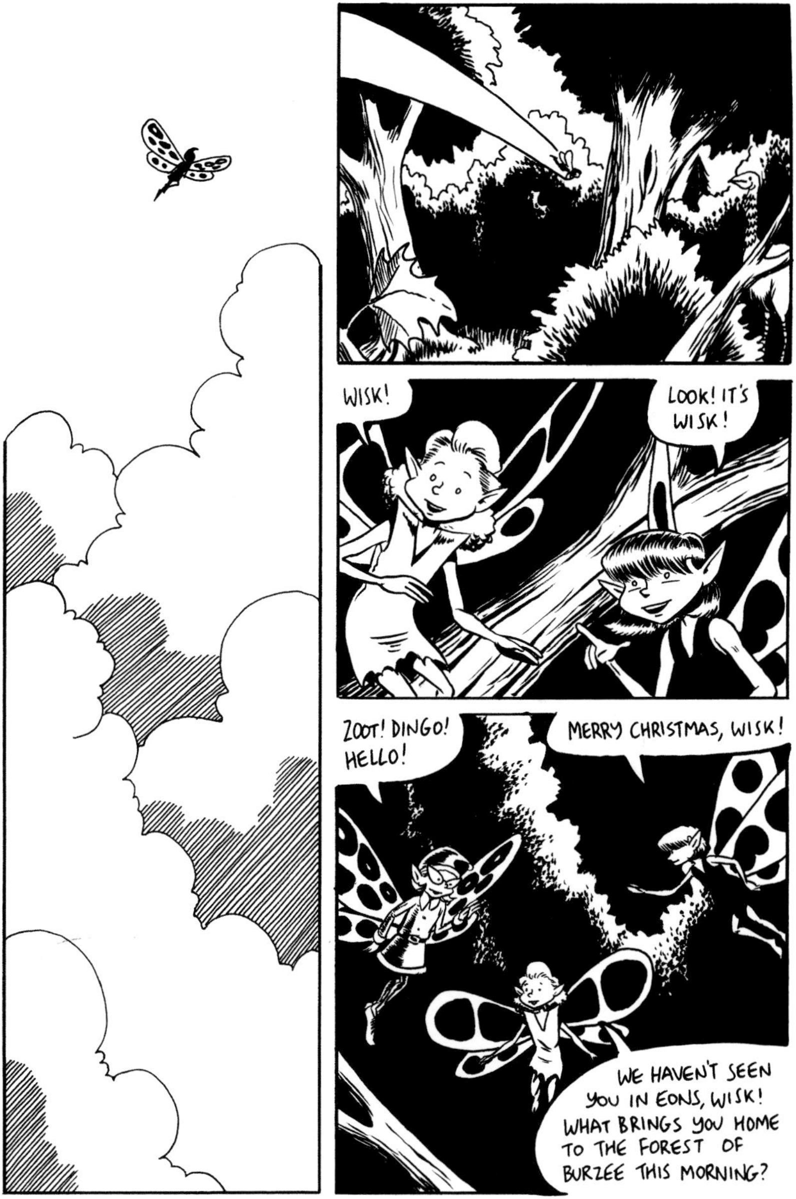
WISK!
LOOK! IT'S WISK!
ZOOT! DINGO! HELLO!
MERRY CHRISTMAS, WISK!
WE HAVEN'T SEEN YOU IN EONS, WISK! WHAT BRINGS YOU HOME TO THE FOREST OF BURZEE THIS MORNING?

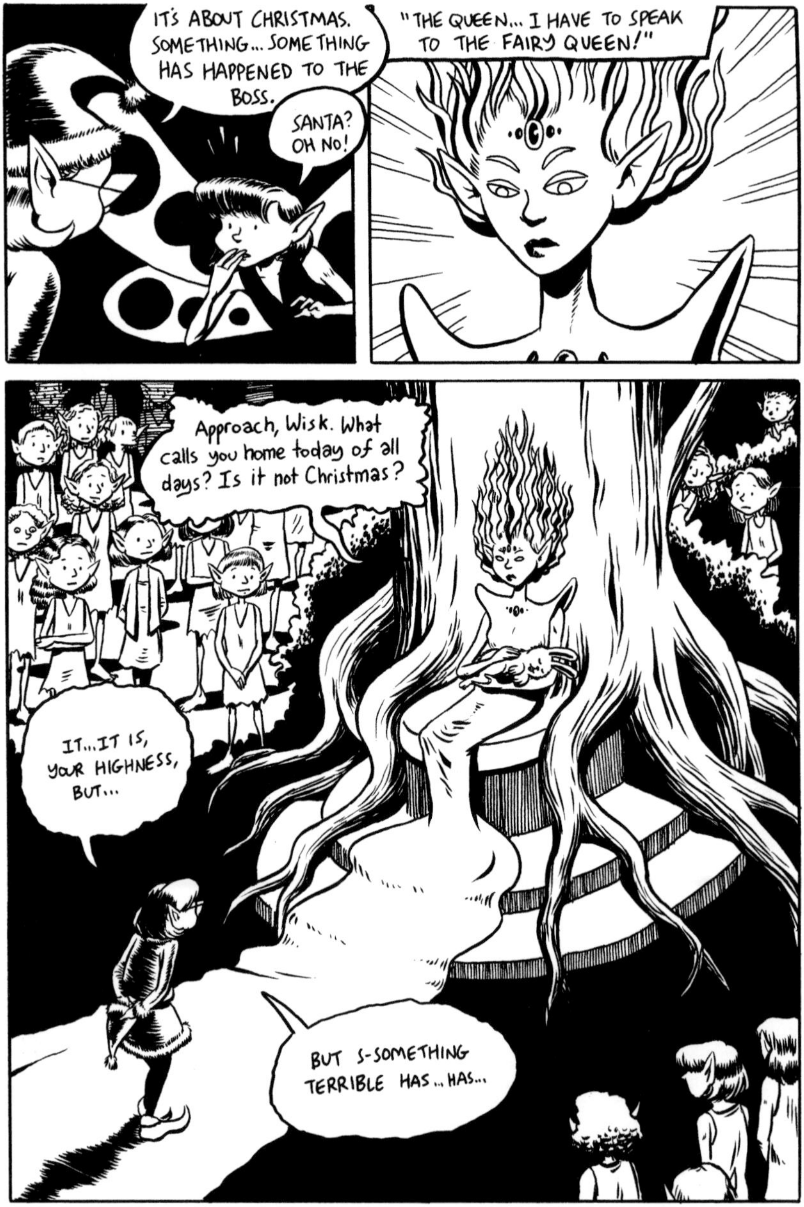
IT'S ABOUT CHRISTMAS. SOMETHING... SOMETHING HAS HAPPENED TO THE BOSS.
SANTA? OH NO!
"THE QUEEN... I HAVE TO SPEAK TO THE FAIRY QUEEN!"
Approach, Wisk. What calls you home today of all days? Is it not Christmas?
IT...IT IS, YOUR HIGHNESS, BUT...
BUT S-SOMETHING TERRIBLE HAS... HAS...

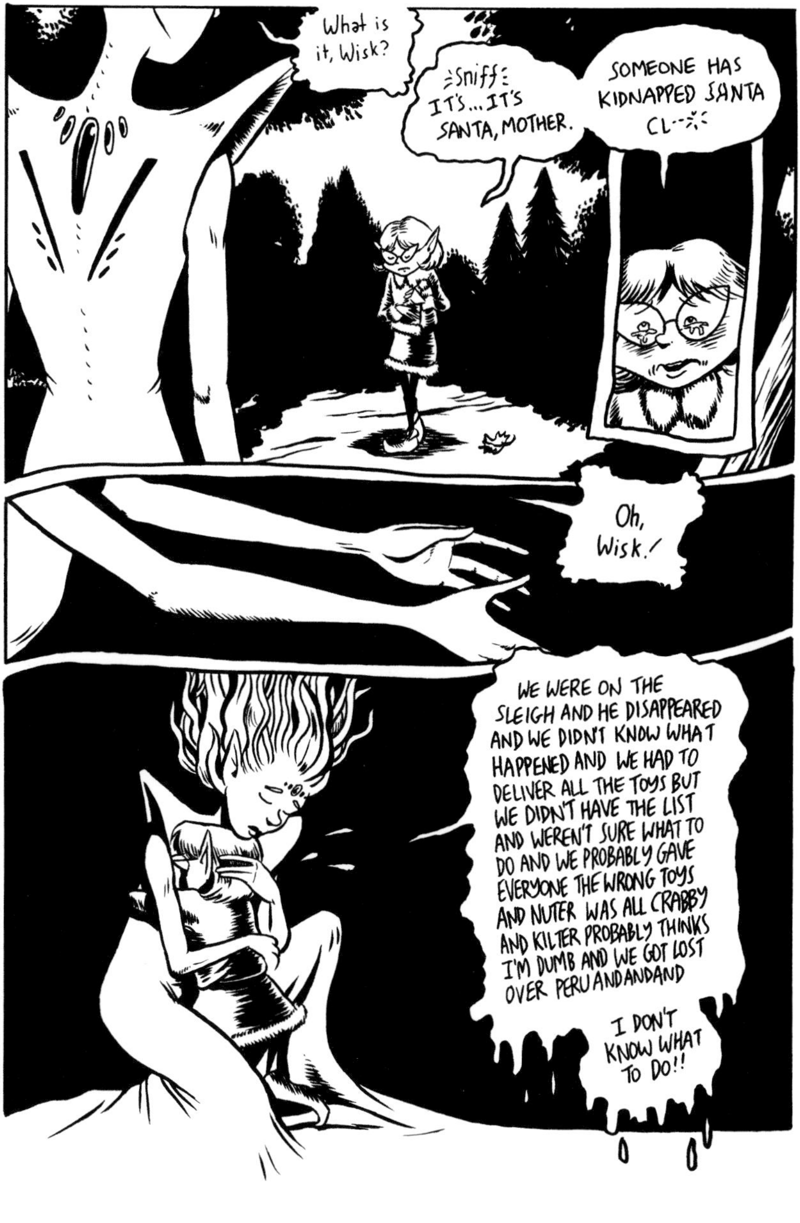

What is it, Wisk?
Sniff IT'S... IT'S SANTA, MOTHER.
SOMEONE HAS KIDNAPPED SANTA CL--
Oh, Wisk!
WE WERE ON THE SLEIGH AND HE DISAPPEARED AND WE DIDN'T KNOW WHAT HAPPENED AND WE HAD TO DELIVER ALL THE TOYS BUT WE DIDN'T HAVE THE LIST AND WEREN'T SURE WHAT TO DO AND WE PROBABLY GAVE EVERYONE THE WRONG TOYS AND NUTER WAS ALL CRABBY AND KILTER PROBABLY THINKS I'M DUMB AND WE GOT LOST OVER PERU ANDANDAND
I DON'T KNOW WHAT TO DO!!

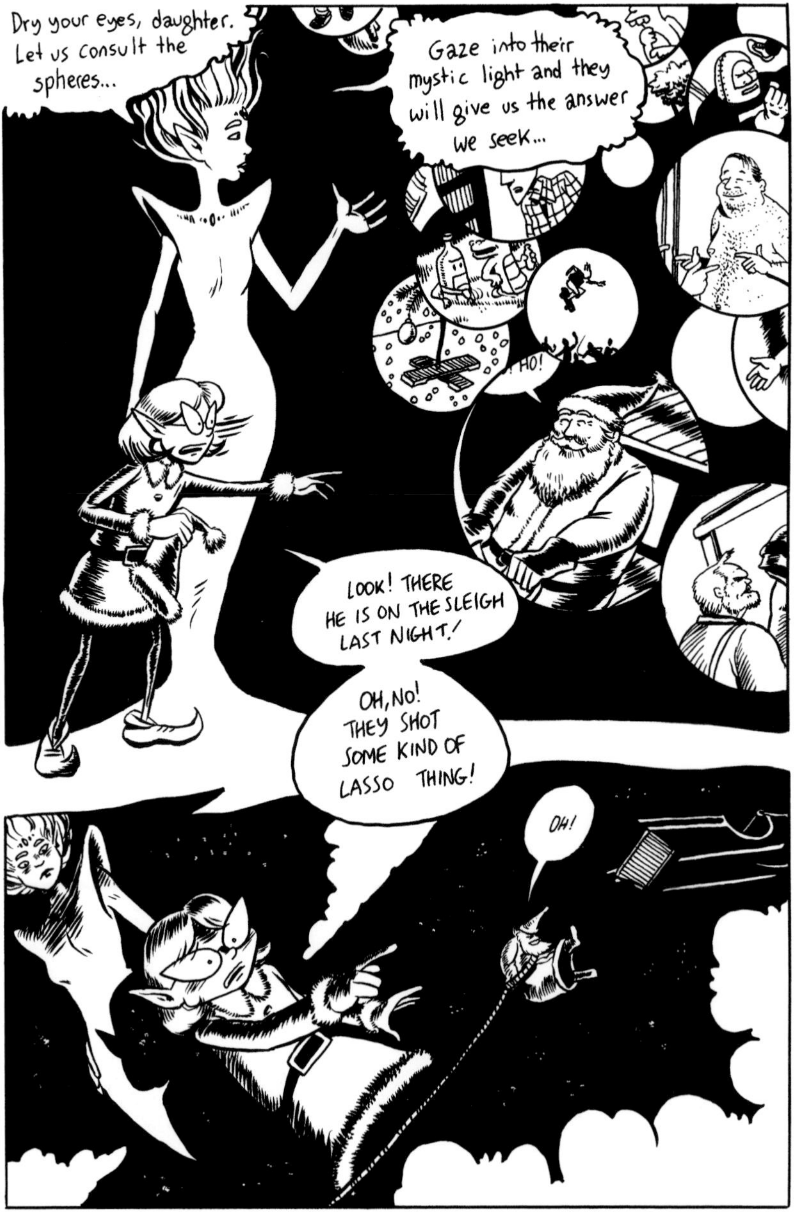
Dry your eyes, daughter. Let us consult the spheres...
Gaze into their mystic light and they will give us the answer we seek...
HO!
LOOK! THERE HE IS ON THE SLEIGH LAST NIGHT!
OH, NO! THEY SHOT SOME KIND OF LASSO THING!
OH!

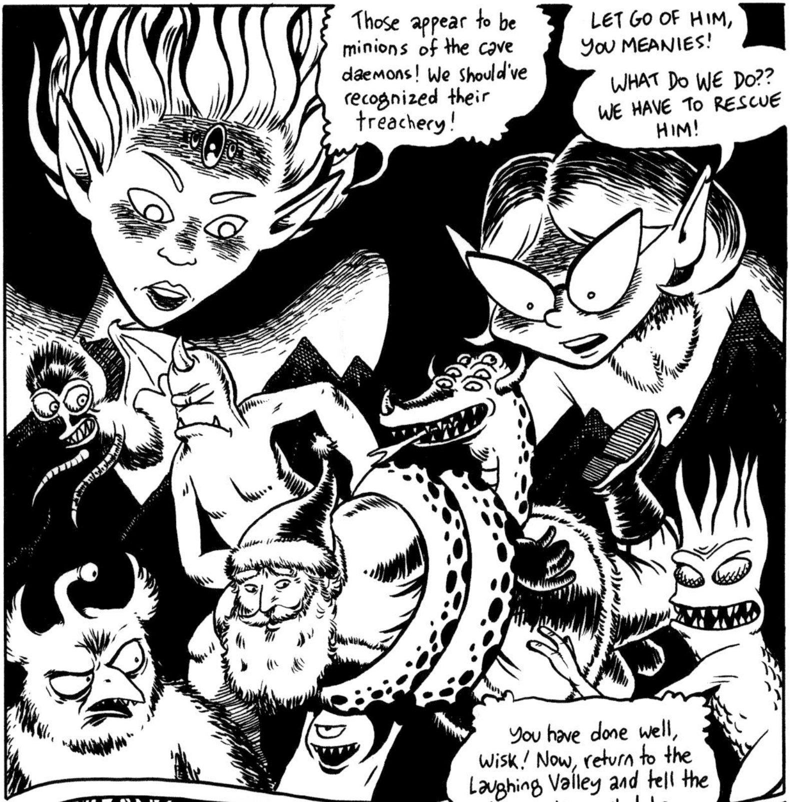
Those appear to be minions of the cave daemons! We should've recognized their treachery!
LET GO OF HIM, YOU MEANIES!
WHAT DO WE DO?? WE HAVE TO RESCUE HIM!

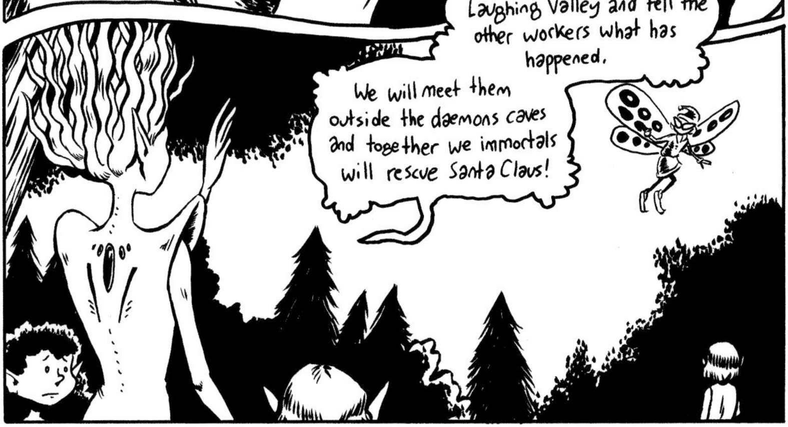
You have done well, Wisk! Now, return to the Laughing Valley and tell the other workers what has happened.
We will meet them outside the daemons caves and together we immortals will rescue Santa Claus!

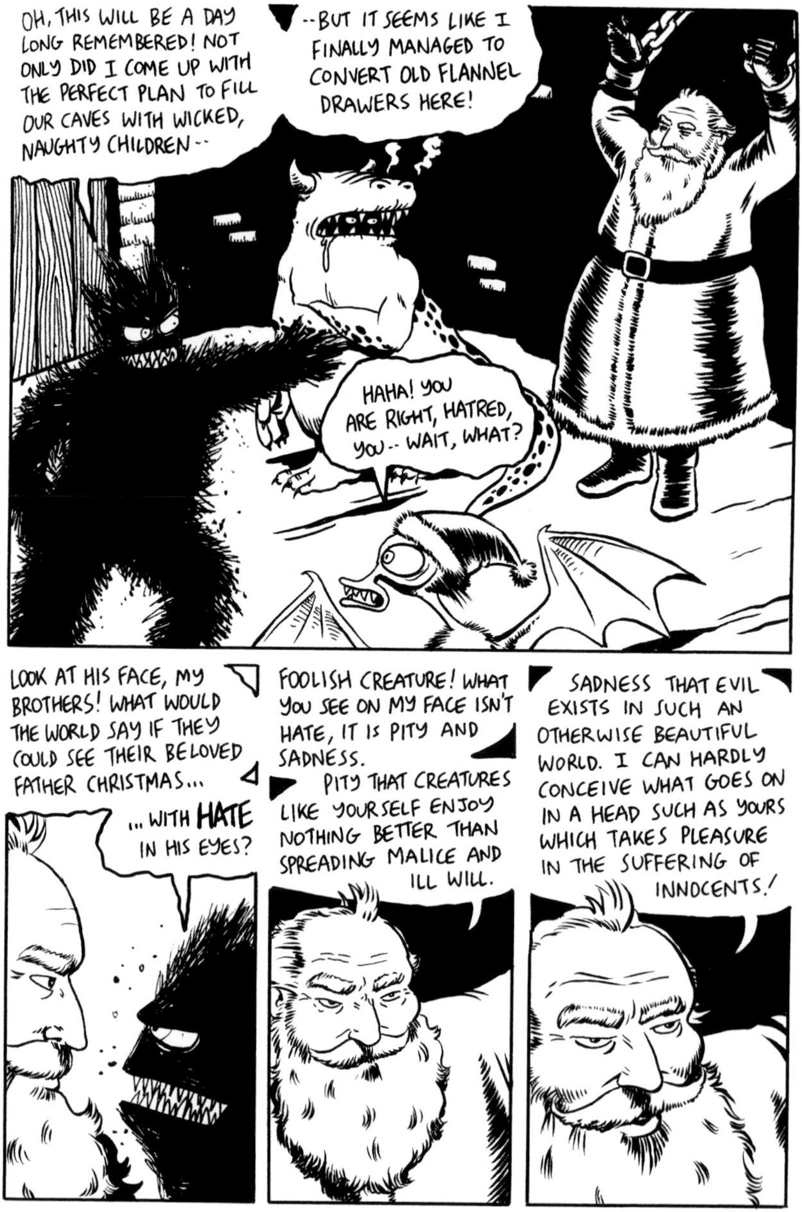
OH, THIS WILL BE A DAY LONG REMEMBERED! NOT ONLY DID I COME UP WITH THE PERFECT PLAN TO FILL OUR CAVES WITH WICKED, NAUGHTY CHILDREN--
--BUT IT SEEMS LIKE I FINALLY MANAGED TO CONVERT OLD FLANNEL DRAWERS HERE!
HAHA! YOU ARE RIGHT, HATRED, YOU-- WAIT, WHAT?
LOOK AT HIS FACE, MY BROTHERS! WHAT WOULD THE WORLD SAY IF THEY COULD SEE THEIR BELOVED FATHER CHRISTMAS...
...WITH HATE IN HIS EYES?
FOOLISH CREATURE! WHAT YOU SEE ON MY FACE ISN'T HATE, IT IS PITY AND SADNESS.
PITY THAT CREATURES LIKE YOURSELF ENJOY NOTHING BETTER THAN SPREADING MALICE AND ILL WILL.
SADNESS THAT EVIL EXISTS IN SUCH AN OTHERWISE BEAUTIFUL WORLD. I CAN HARDLY CONCEIVE WHAT GOES ON IN A HEAD SUCH AS YOURS WHICH TAKES PLEASURE IN THE SUFFERING OF INNOCENTS!

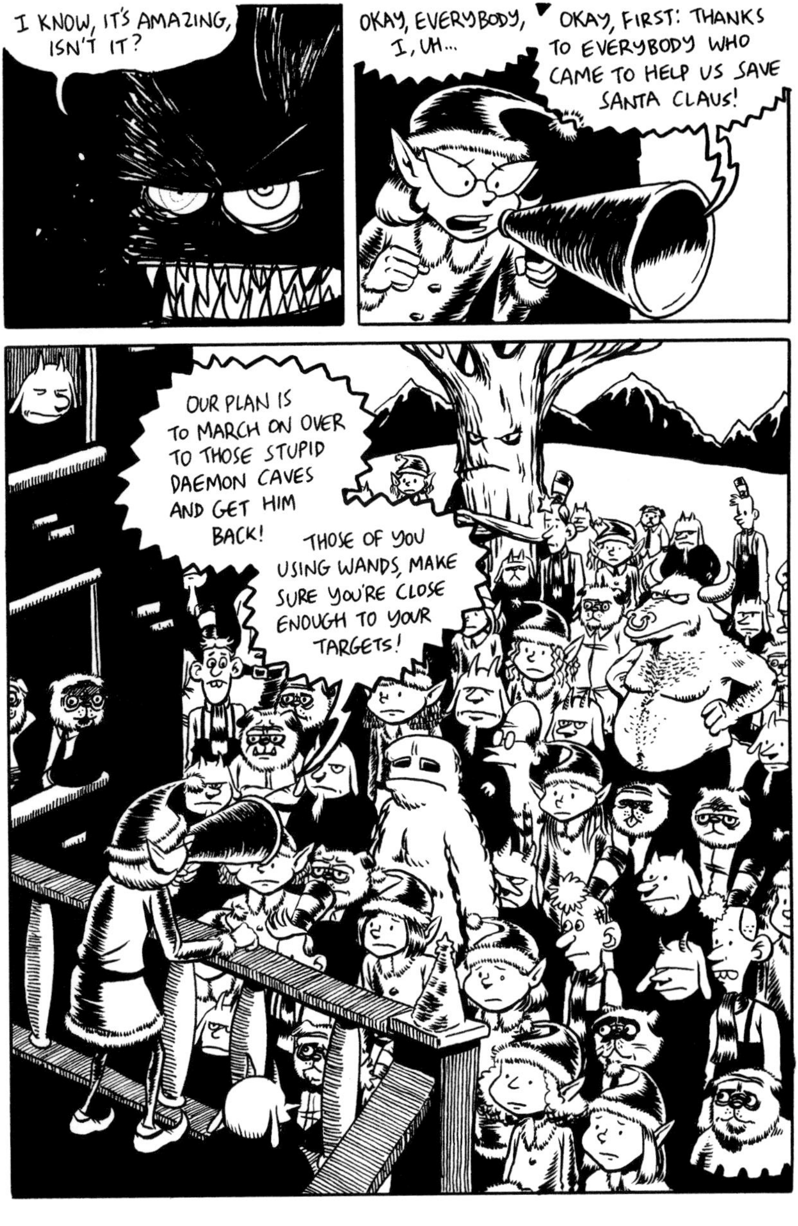
I KNOW, IT'S AMAZING, ISN'T IT?
OKAY, EVERYBODY, I, UH...
OKAY, FIRST: THANKS TO EVERYBODY WHO CAME TO HELP US SAVE SANTA CLAUS!
OUR PLAN IS TO MARCH ON OVER TO THOSE STUPID DAEMON CAVES AND GET HIM BACK!
THOSE OF YOU USING WANDS, MAKE SURE YOU'RE CLOSE ENOUGH TO YOUR TARGETS!

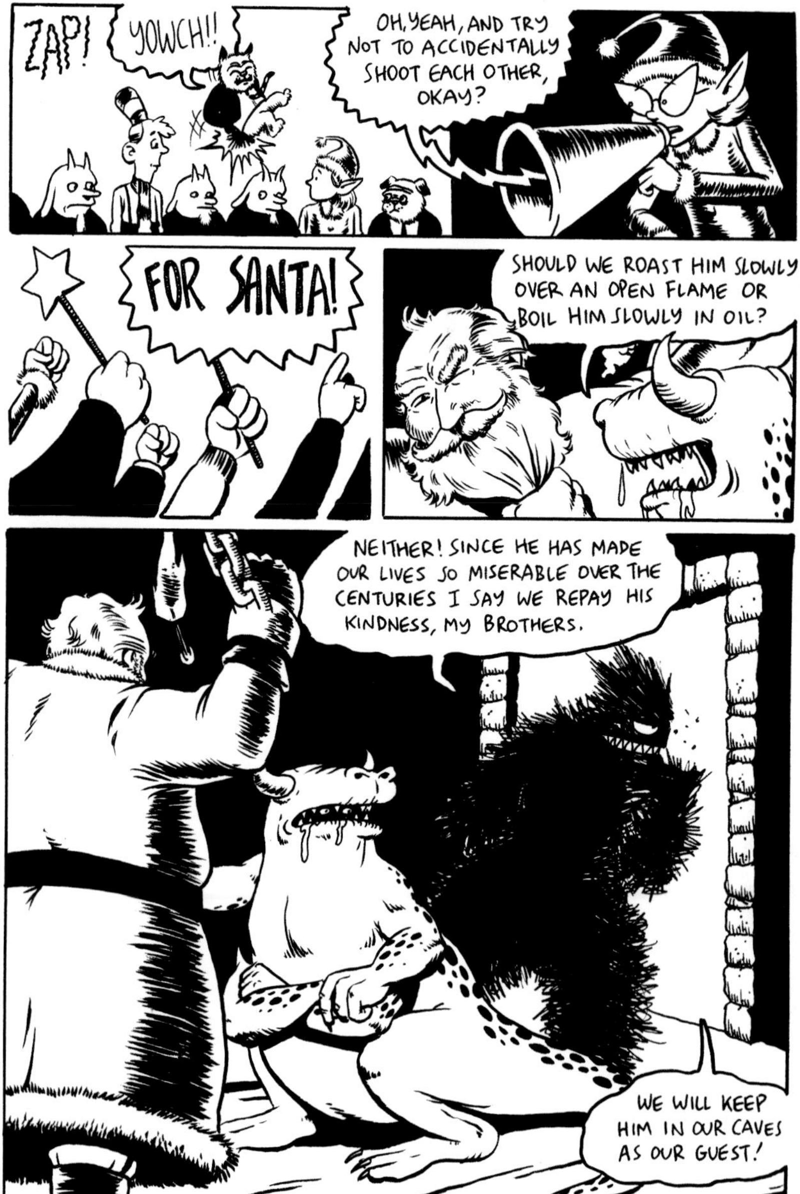
ZAP!
YOWCH!!
OH, YEAH, AND TRY NOT TO ACCIDENTALLY SHOOT EACH OTHER, OKAY?
FOR SANTA!
SHOULD WE ROAST HIM SLOWLY OVER AN OPEN FLAME OR BOIL HIM SLOWLY IN OIL?
NEITHER! SINCE HE HAS MADE OUR LIVES SO MISERABLE OVER THE CENTURIES I SAY WE REPAY HIS KINDNESS, MY BROTHERS.
WE WILL KEEP HIM IN OUR CAVES AS OUR GUEST!

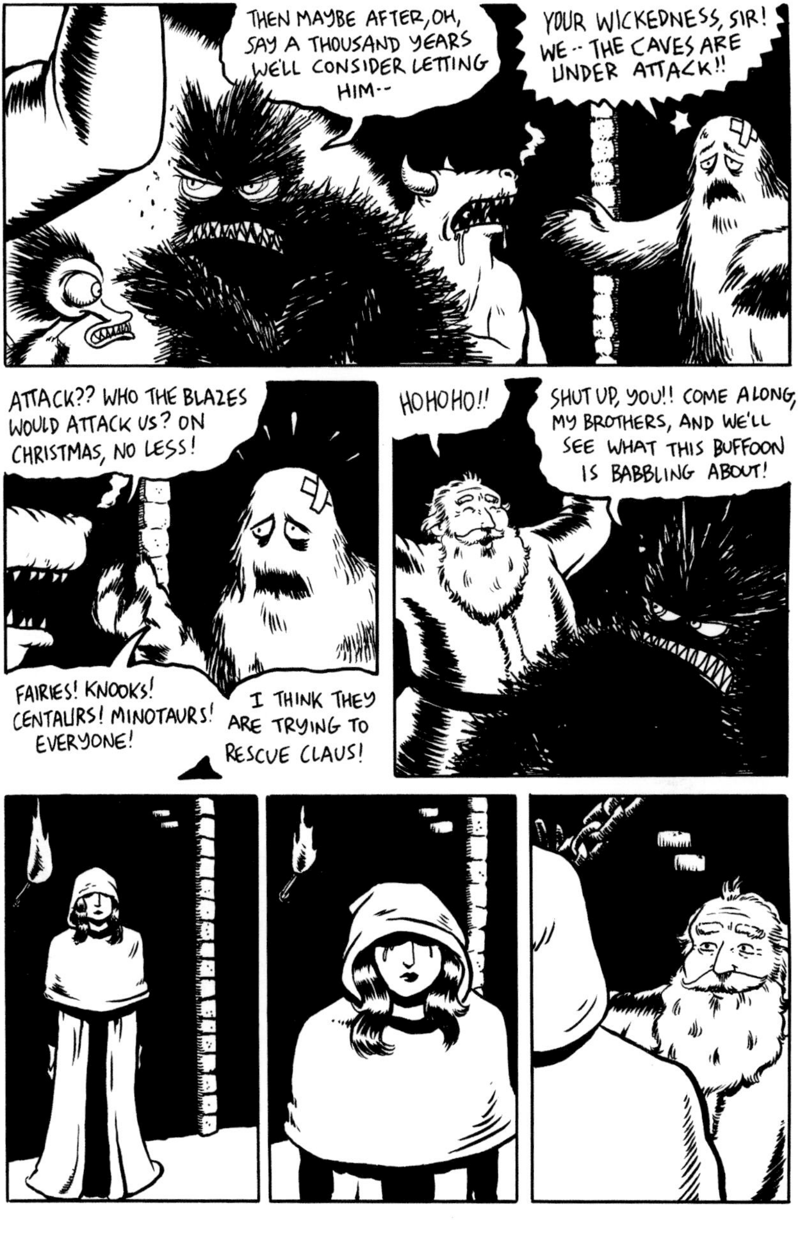
THEN MAYBE AFTER, OH, SAY A THOUSAND YEARS WE'LL CONSIDER LETTING HIM--
YOUR WICKEDNESS, SIR! WE-- THE CAVES ARE UNDER ATTACK!!
ATTACK?? WHO THE BLAZES WOULD ATTACK US? ON CHRISTMAS, NO LESS!
FAIRIES! KNOOKS! CENTAURS! MINOTAURS! EVERYONE!
I THINK THEY ARE TRYING TO RESCUE CLAUS!
HOHOHO!!
SHUT UP, YOU!! COME ALONG, MY BROTHERS, AND WE'LL SEE WHAT THIS BUFFOON IS BABBLING ABOUT!

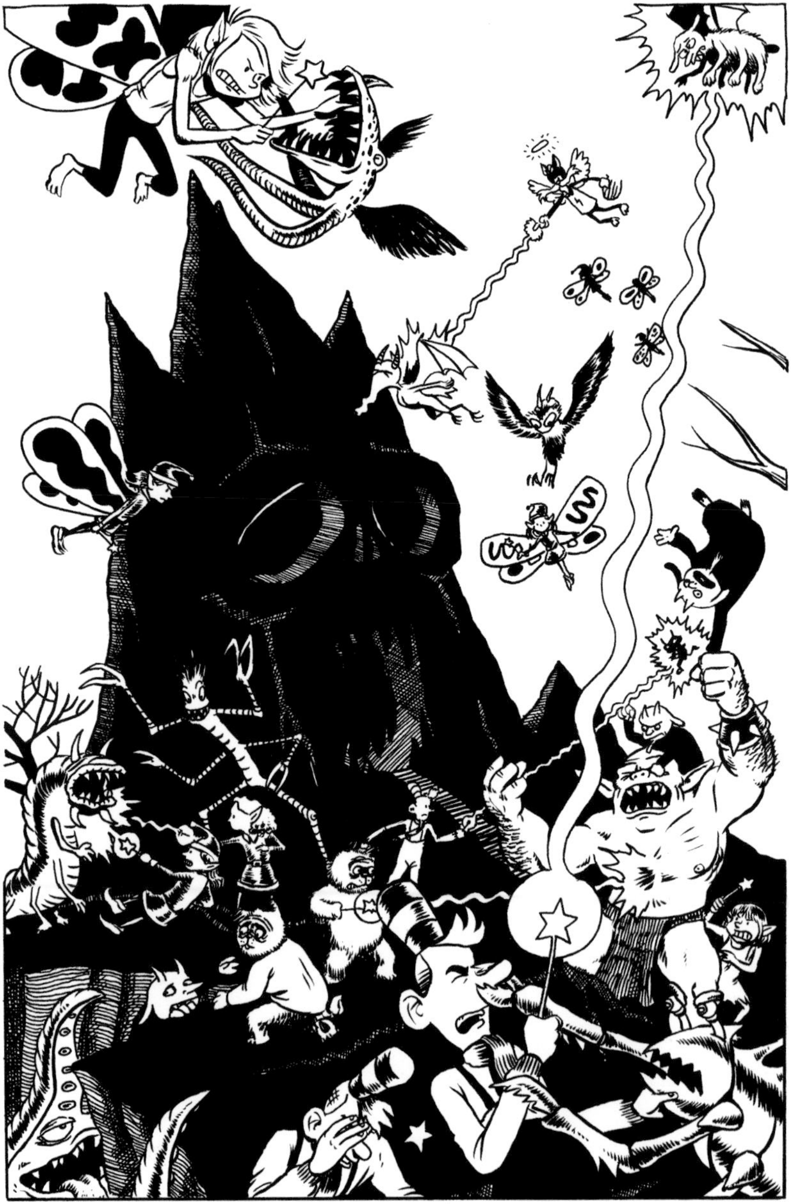

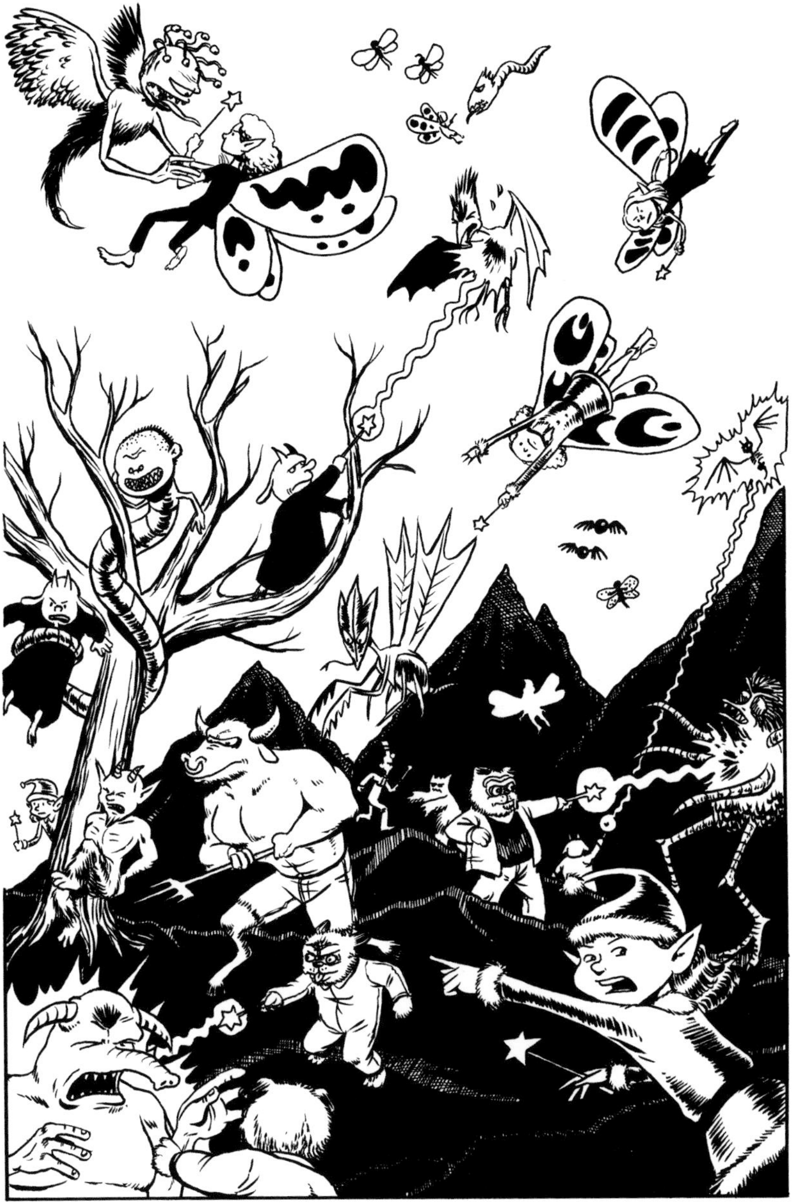

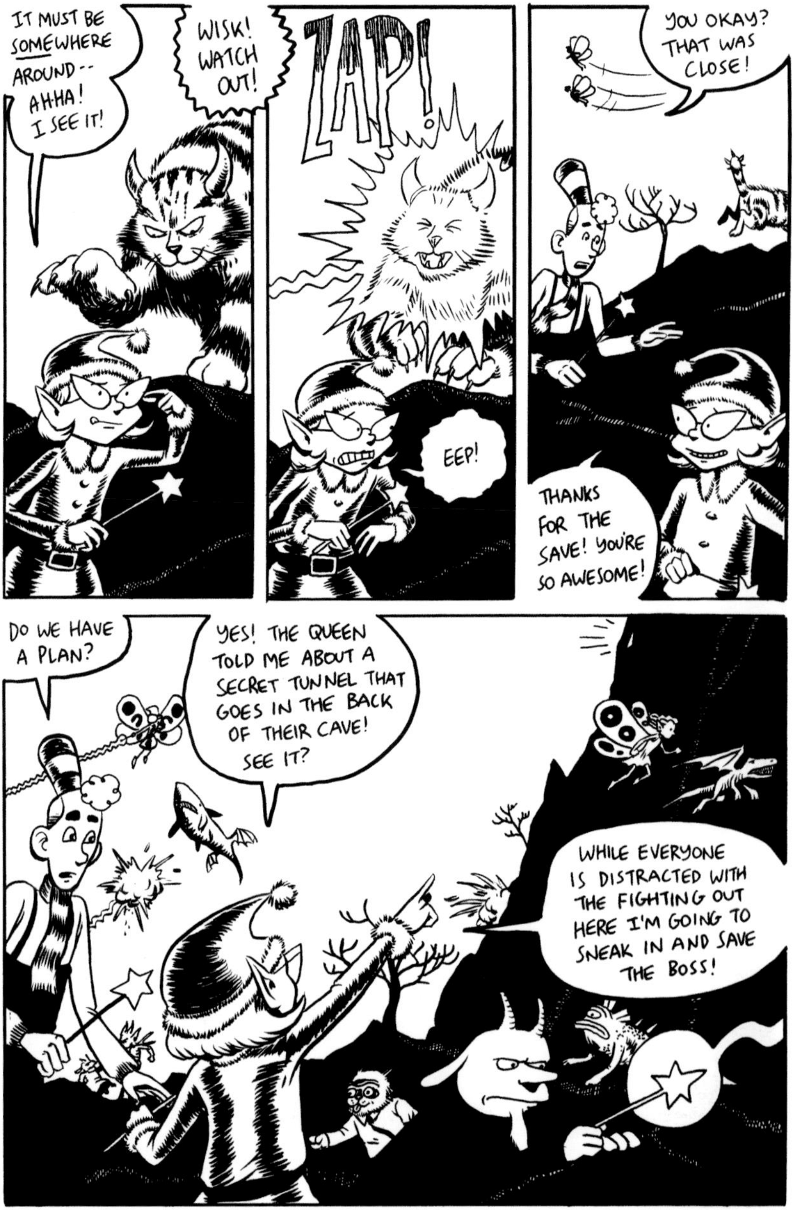
IT MUST BE SOMEWHERE AROUND-- AHHA! I SEE IT!
WISK! WATCH OUT!
ZAP!
EEP!
YOU OKAY? THAT WAS CLOSE!
THANKS FOR THE SAVE! YOU'RE SO AWESOME!
DO WE HAVE A PLAN?
YES! THE QUEEN TOLD ME ABOUT A SECRET TUNNEL THAT GOES IN THE BACK OF THEIR CAVE! SEE IT?
WHILE EVERYONE IS DISTRACTED WITH THE FIGHTING OUT HERE I'M GOING TO SNEAK IN AND SAVE THE BOSS!

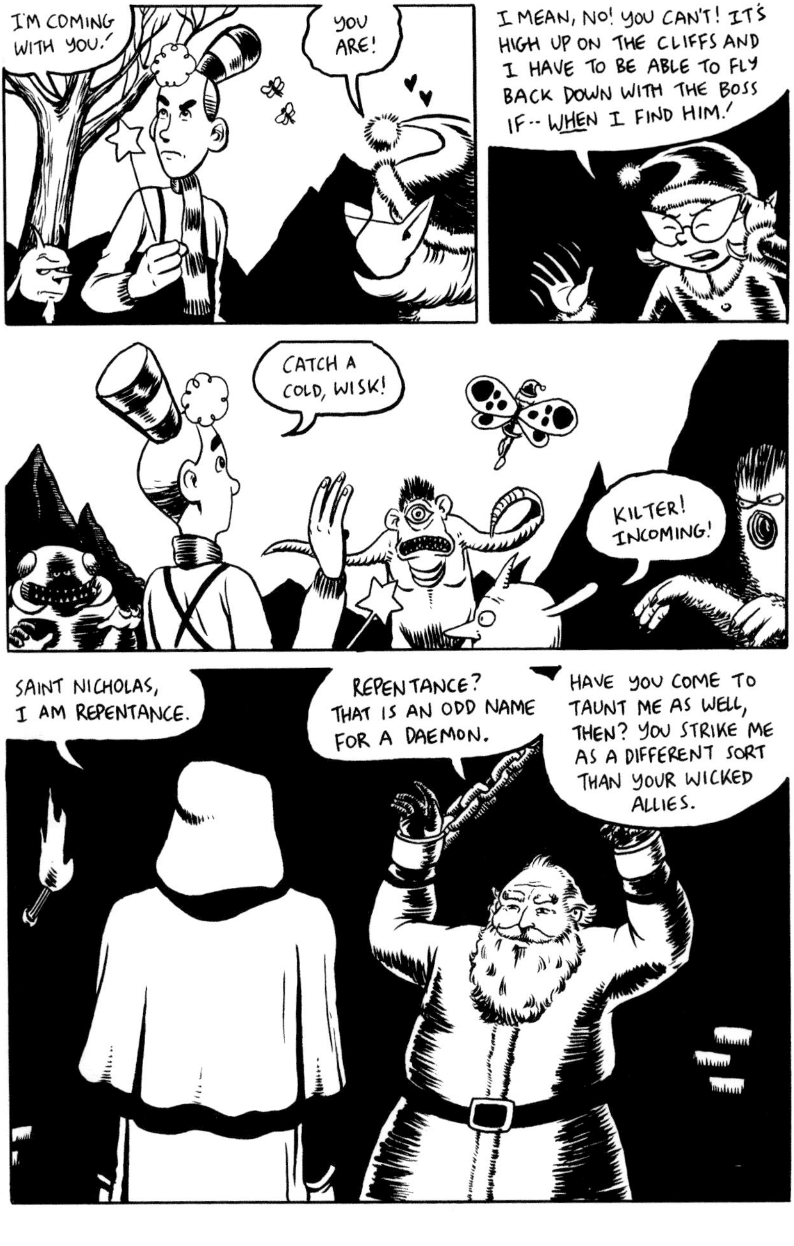
I'M COMING WITH YOU!
YOU ARE!
I MEAN, NO! YOU CAN'T! IT'S HIGH UP ON THE CLIFFS AND I HAVE TO BE ABLE TO FLY BACK DOWN WITH THE BOSS IF-- WHEN I FIND HIM!
CATCH A COLD, WISK!
KILTER! INCOMING!
SAINT NICHOLAS, I AM REPENTANCE.
REPENTANCE? THAT IS AN ODD NAME FOR A DAEMON.
HAVE YOU COME TO TAUNT ME AS WELL, THEN? YOU STRIKE ME AS A DIFFERENT SORT THAN YOUR WICKED ALLIES.

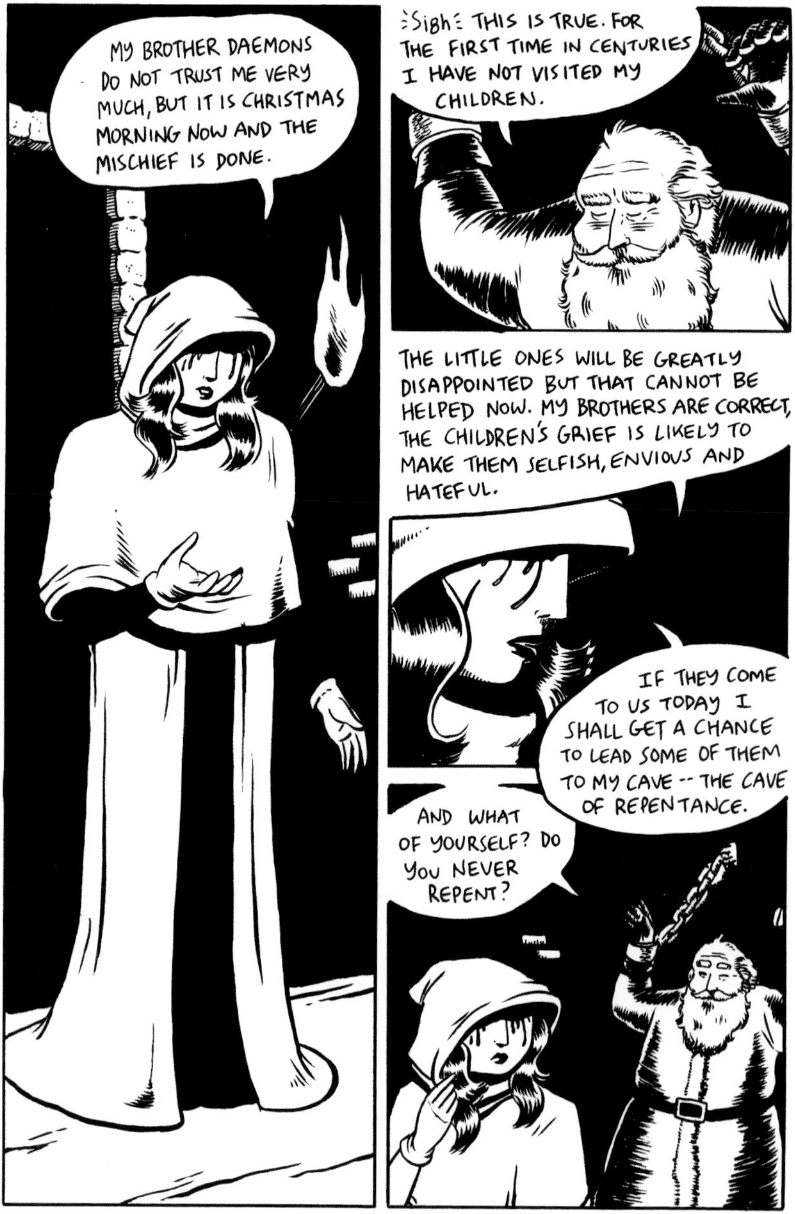
MY BROTHER DAEMONS DO NOT TRUST ME VERY MUCH, BUT IT IS CHRISTMAS MORNING NOW AND THE MISCHIEF IS DONE.
:SIGH: THIS IS TRUE. FOR THE FIRST TIME IN CENTURIES I HAVE NOT VISITED MY CHILDREN.
THE LITTLE ONES WILL BE GREATLY DISAPPOINTED BUT THAT CANNOT BE HELPED NOW. MY BROTHERS ARE CORRECT, THE CHILDREN'S GRIEF IS LIKELY TO MAKE THEM SELFISH, ENVIOUS AND HATEFUL.
IF THEY COME TO US TODAY I SHALL GET A CHANCE TO LEAD SOME OF THEM TO MY CAVE -- THE CAVE OF REPENTANCE.
AND WHAT OF YOURSELF? DO YOU NEVER REPENT?

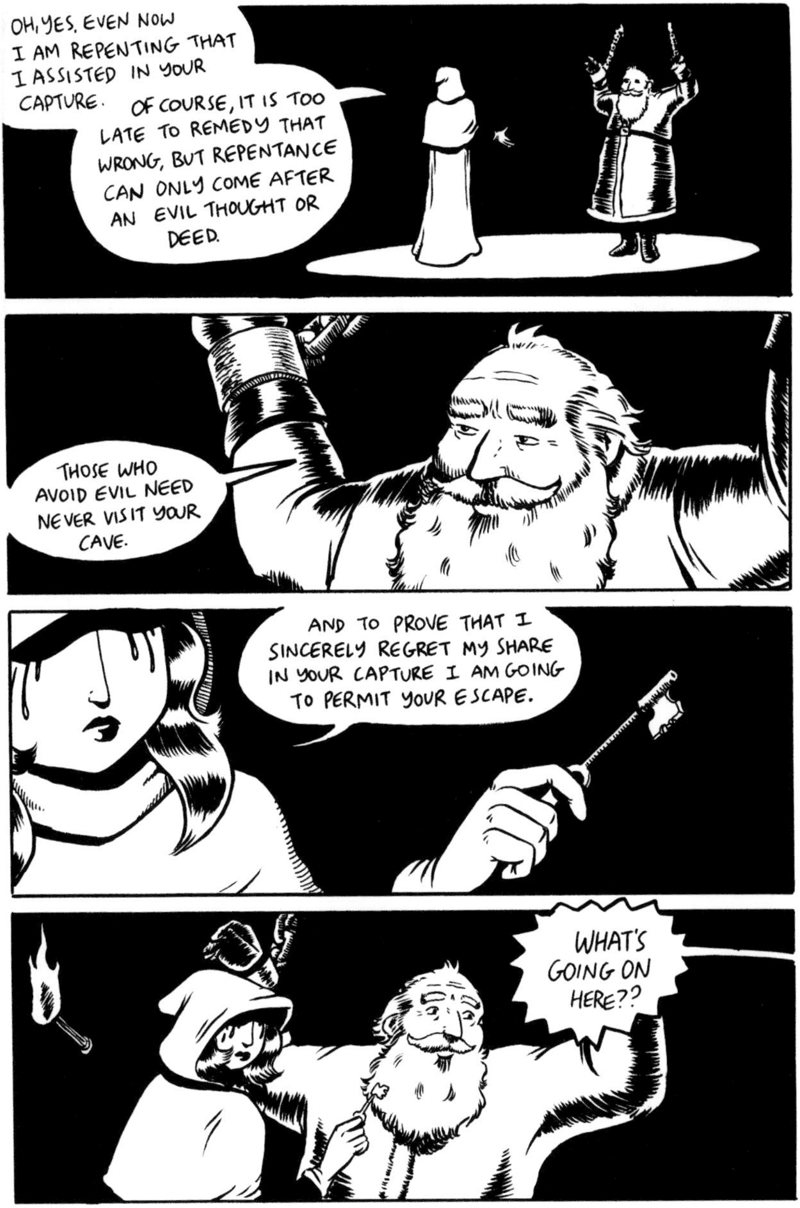
OH, YES. EVEN NOW I AM REPENTING THAT I ASSISTED IN YOUR CAPTURE.
OF COURSE, IT IS TOO LATE TO REMEDY THAT WRONG, BUT REPENTANCE CAN ONLY COME AFTER AN EVIL THOUGHT OR DEED.
THOSE WHO AVOID EVIL NEED NEVER VISIT YOUR CAVE.
AND TO PROVE THAT I SINCERELY REGRET MY SHARE IN YOUR CAPTURE I AM GOING TO PERMIT YOUR ESCAPE.
WHAT'S GOING ON HERE??

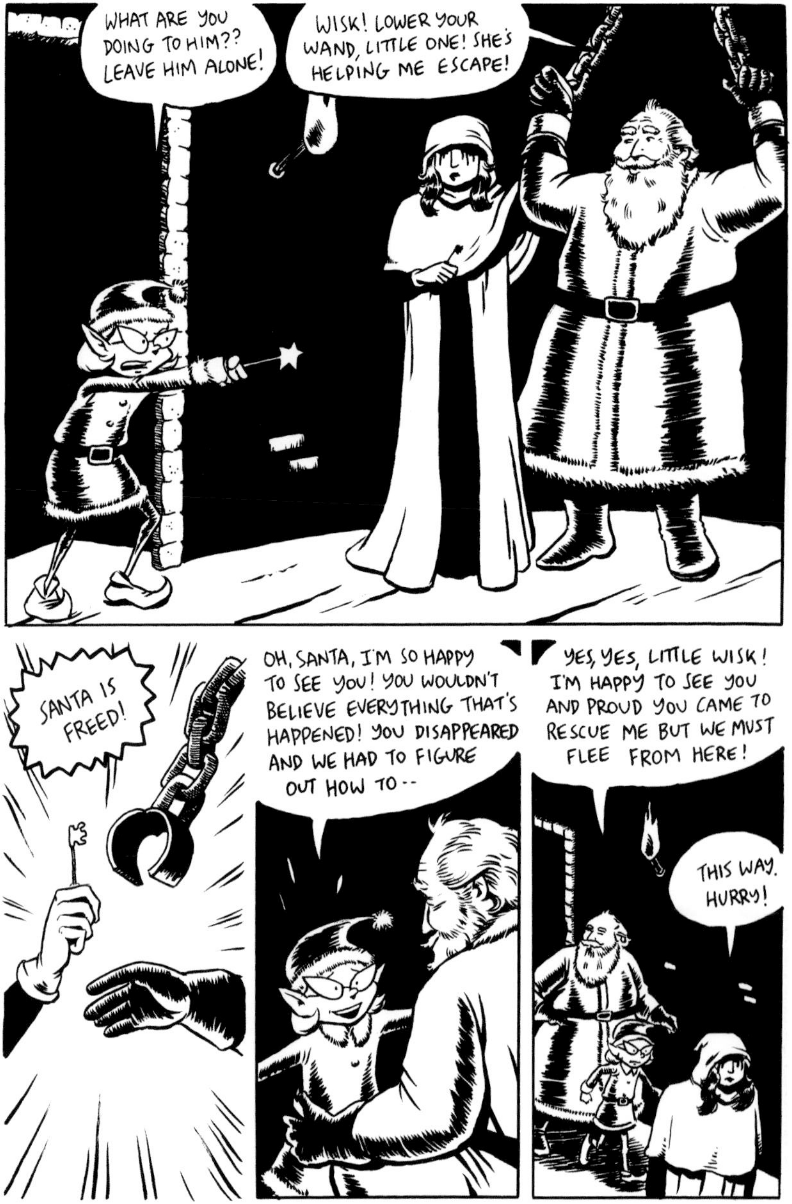
WHAT ARE YOU DOING TO HIM?? LEAVE HIM ALONE!
WISK! LOWER YOUR WAND, LITTLE ONE! SHE'S HELPING ME ESCAPE!
SANTA IS FREED!
OH, SANTA, I'M SO HAPPY TO SEE YOU! YOU WOULDN'T BELIEVE EVERYTHING THAT'S HAPPENED! YOU DISAPPEARED AND WE HAD TO FIGURE OUT HOW TO--
YES, YES, LITTLE WISK! I'M HAPPY TO SEE YOU AND PROUD YOU CAME TO RESCUE ME BUT WE MUST FLEE FROM HERE!
THIS WAY. HURRY!

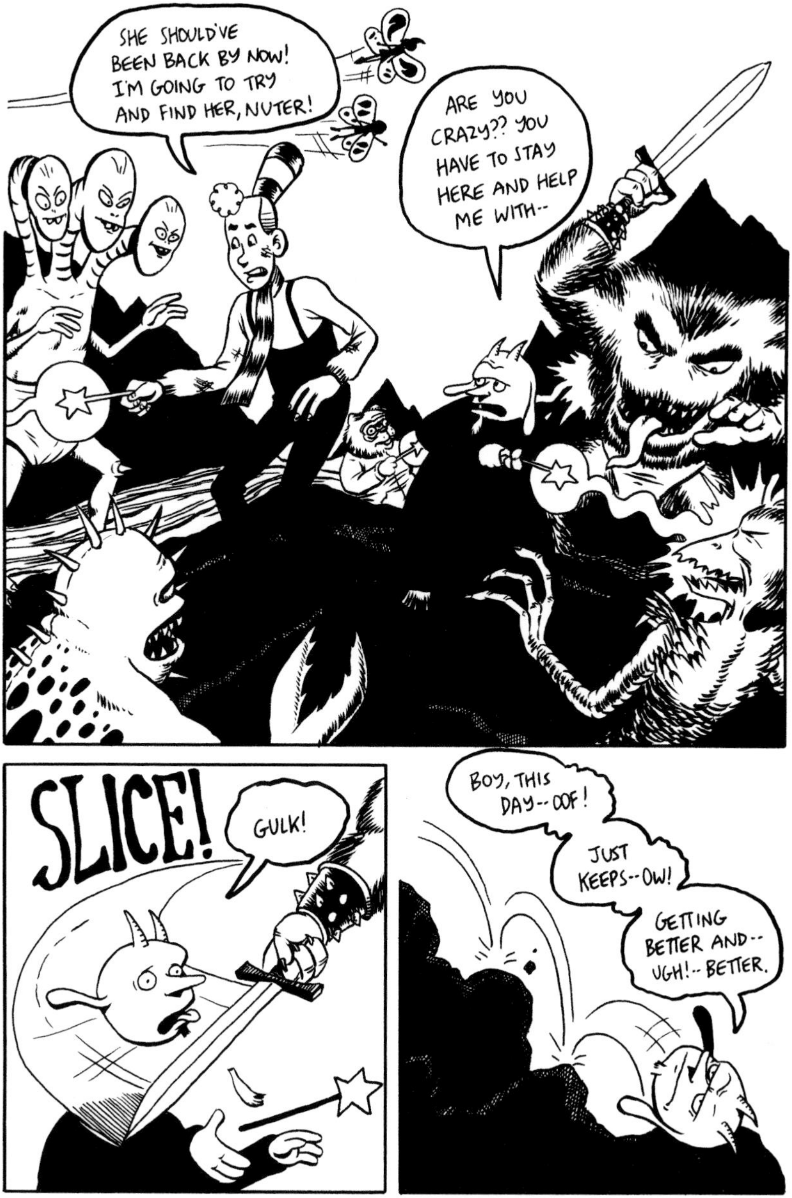
SHE SHOULD'VE BEEN BACK BY NOW! I'M GOING TO TRY AND FIND HER, NUTER!
ARE YOU CRAZY?? YOU HAVE TO STAY HERE AND HELP ME WITH--
SLICE!
GULK!
BOY, THIS DAY--OOF!
JUST KEEPS--OW!
GETTING BETTER AND--UGH!--BETTER.

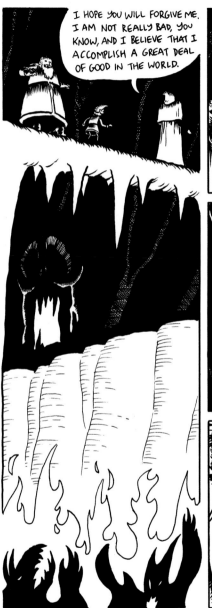

I HOPE YOU WILL FORGIVE ME. I AM NOT REALLY BAD, YOU KNOW, AND I BELIEVE THAT I ACCOMPLISH A GREAT DEAL OF GOOD IN THE WORLD.

YOU HAVE MADE GOOD IN MY EYES, AND I BEAR YOU NO MALICE. I AM SURE THE WORLD WOULD BE A DREARY PLACE WITHOUT--

BOSS! WHAT WAS THAT NOISE?

IF SHE HELPED ANOTHER ONE ESCAPE I'LL KILL HER! C'MON, I THINK I HEAR--

SOMEONE'S COMING!

MY BROTHERS HAVE DISCOVERED YOU ARE FREE. RUN, NICHOLAS. THIS TUNNEL WILL TAKE YOU OUT. I WILL INSURE YOU ARE NOT FOLLOWED.

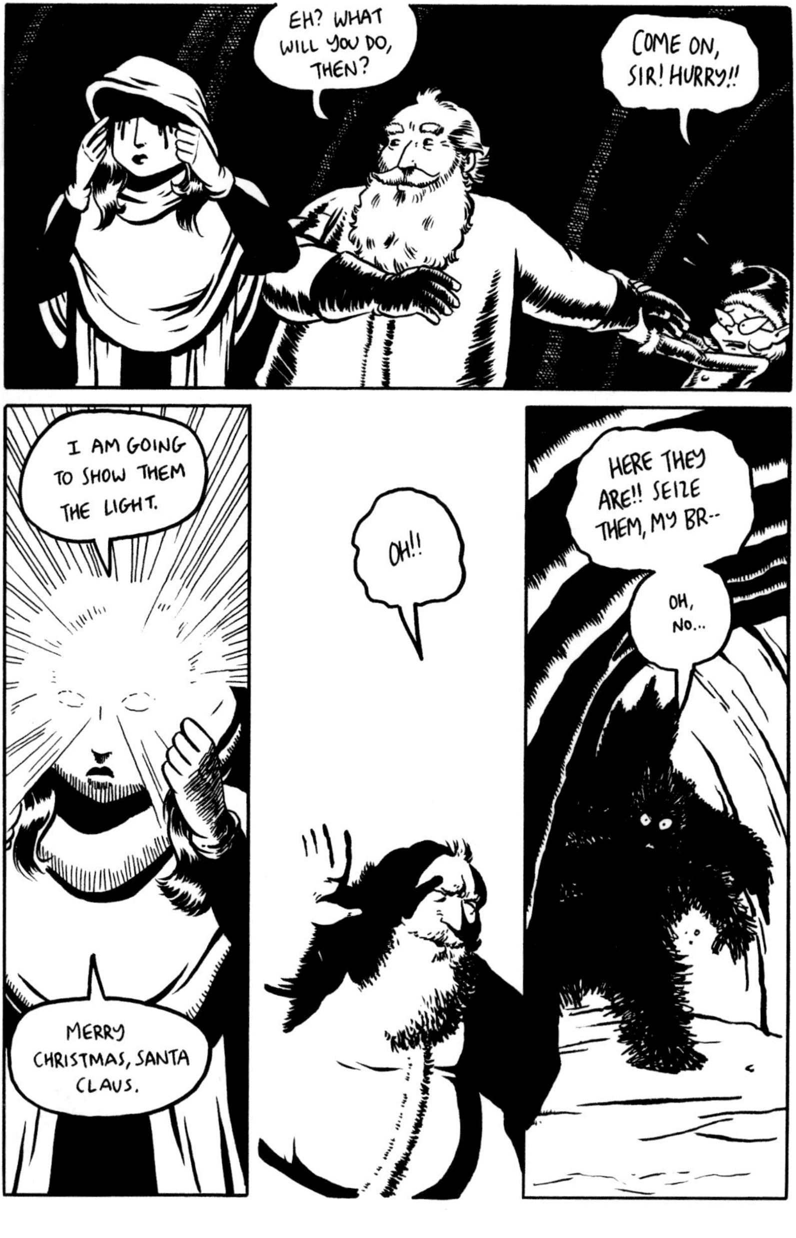

EH? WHAT WILL YOU DO, THEN?
COME ON, SIR! HURRY!!
I AM GOING TO SHOW THEM THE LIGHT.
MERRY CHRISTMAS, SANTA CLAUS.
OH!!
HERE THEY ARE!! SEIZE THEM, MY BR--
OH, NO...

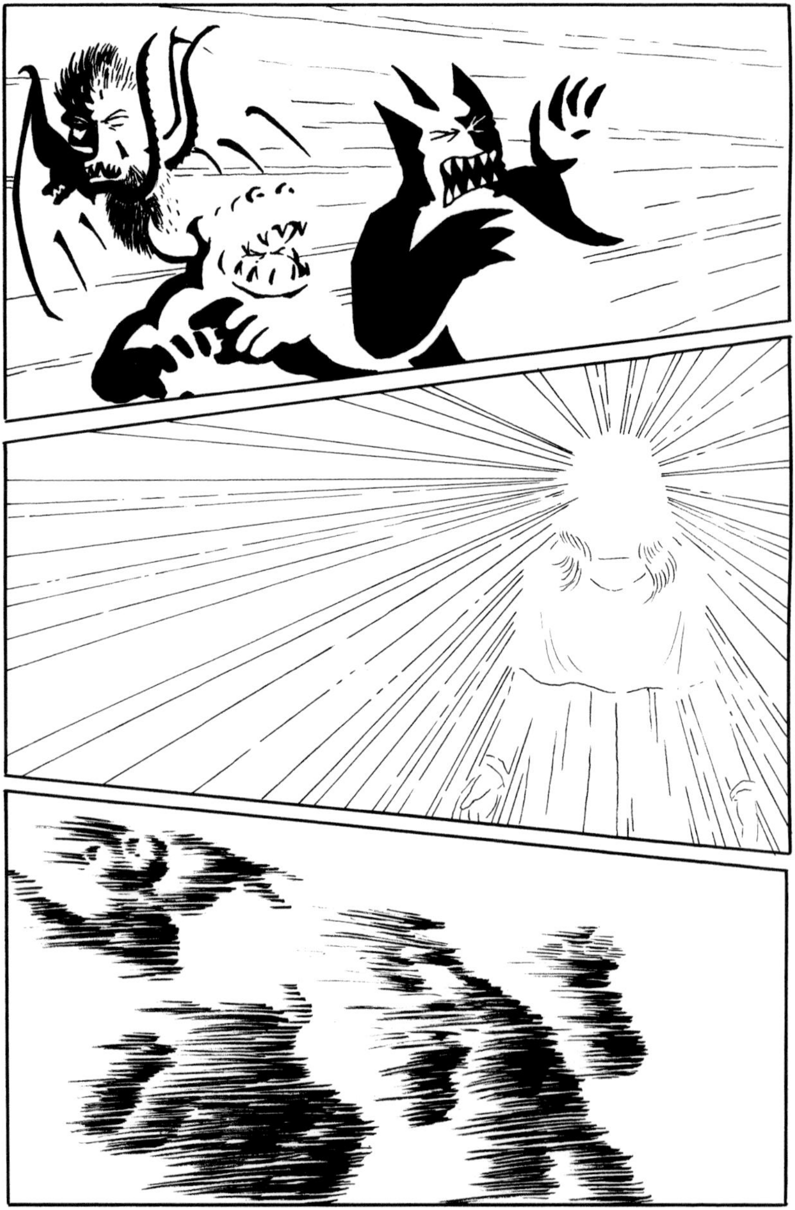

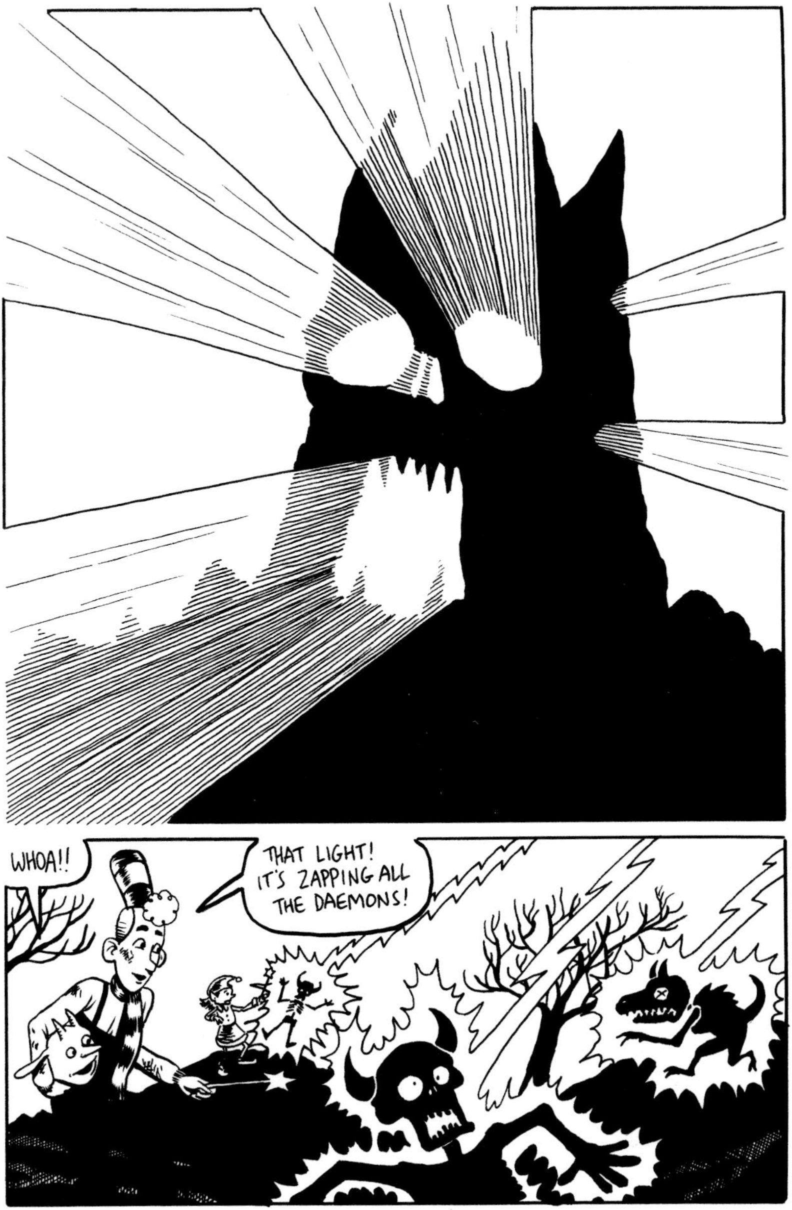
WHOA!!
THAT LIGHT! IT'S ZAPPING ALL THE DAEMONS!

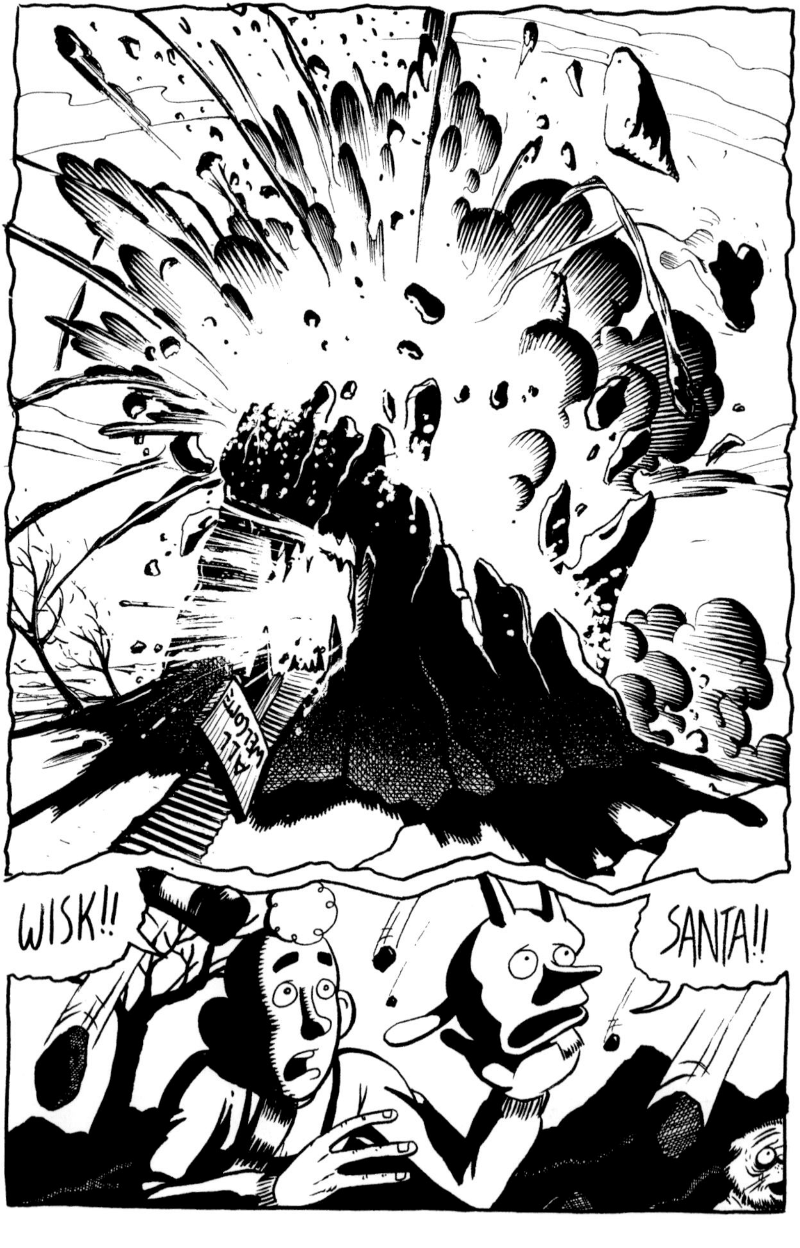
ALL WELCOME
WISK!!
SANTA!!

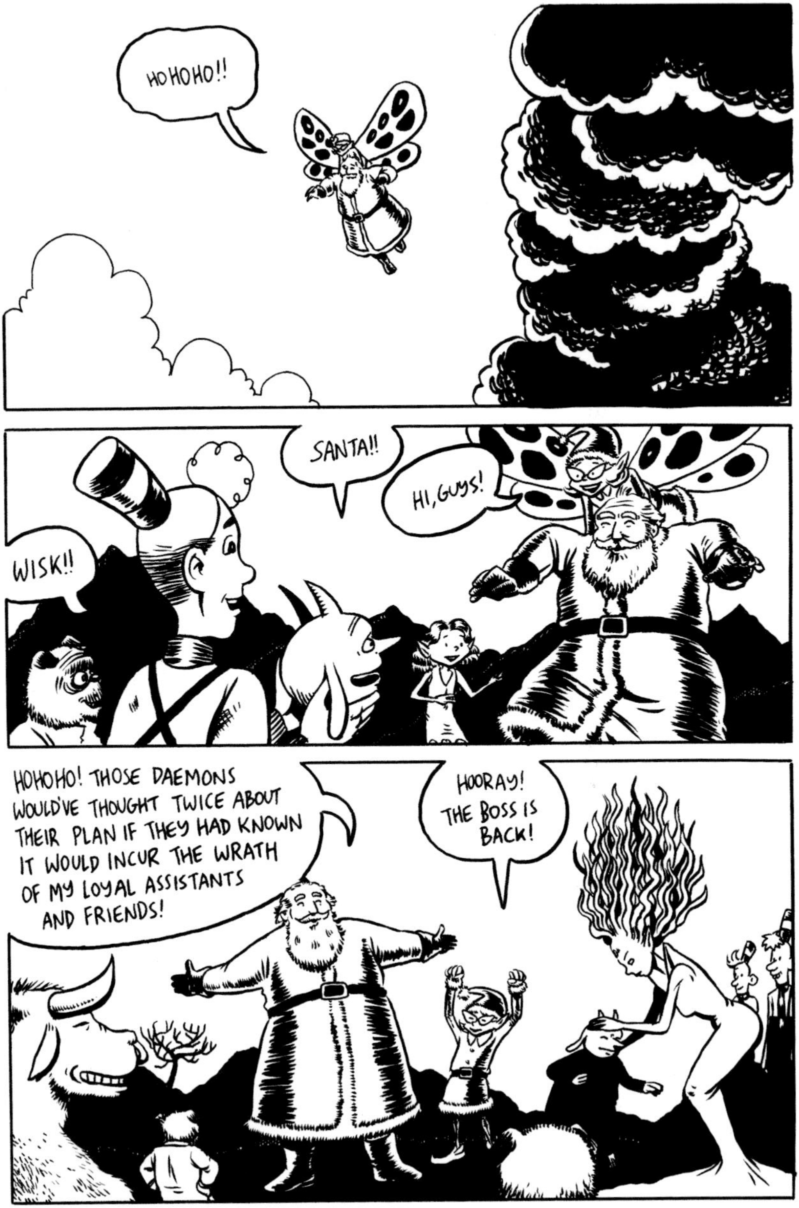
HOHOHO!!
WISK!!
SANTA!!
HI, GUYS!
HOHOHO! THOSE DAEMONS WOULD'VE THOUGHT TWICE ABOUT THEIR PLAN IF THEY HAD KNOWN IT WOULD INCUR THE WRATH OF MY LOYAL ASSISTANTS AND FRIENDS!
HOORAY! THE BOSS IS BACK!

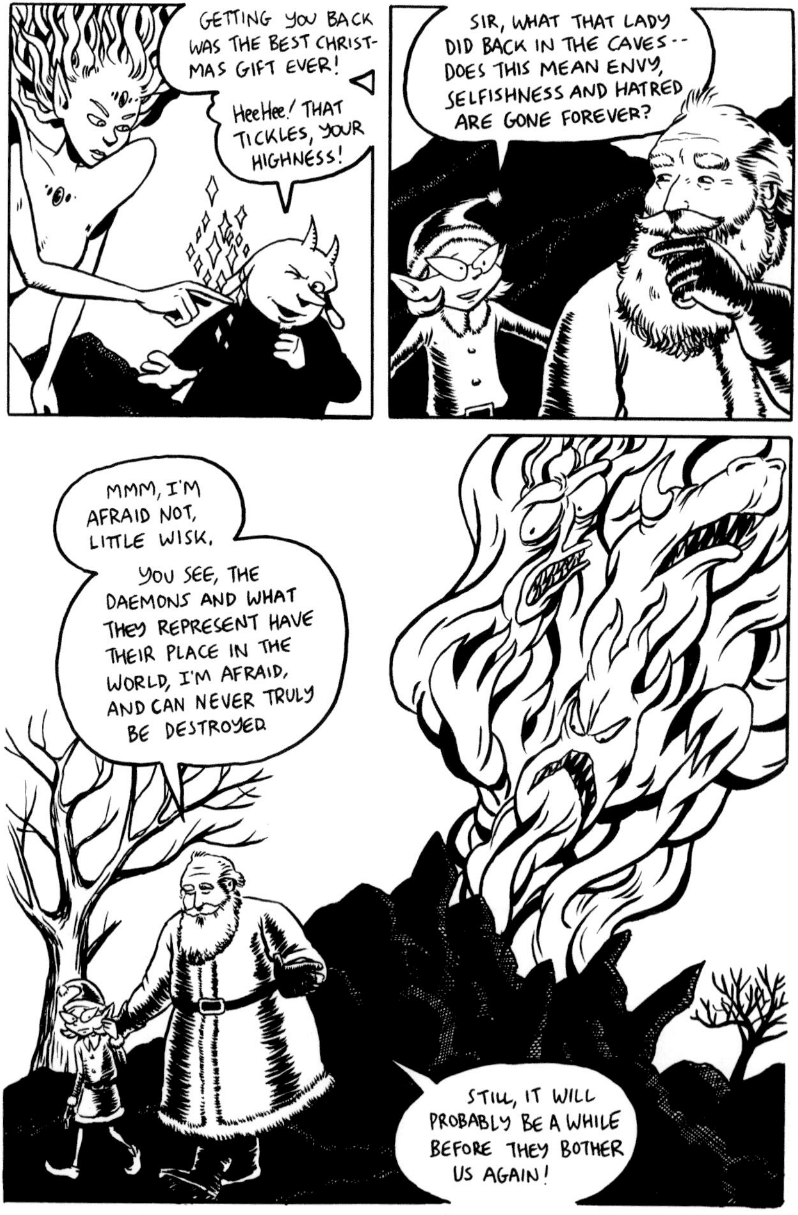
GETTING YOU BACK WAS THE BEST CHRISTMAS GIFT EVER!
HeeHee! THAT TICKLES, YOUR HIGHNESS!
SIR, WHAT THAT LADY DID BACK IN THE CAVES-- DOES THIS MEAN ENVY, SELFISHNESS AND HATRED ARE GONE FOREVER?
MMM, I'M AFRAID NOT, LITTLE WISK.
YOU SEE, THE DAEMONS AND WHAT THEY REPRESENT HAVE THEIR PLACE IN THE WORLD, I'M AFRAID, AND CAN NEVER TRULY BE DESTROYED
STILL, IT WILL PROBABLY BE A WHILE BEFORE THEY BOTHER US AGAIN!

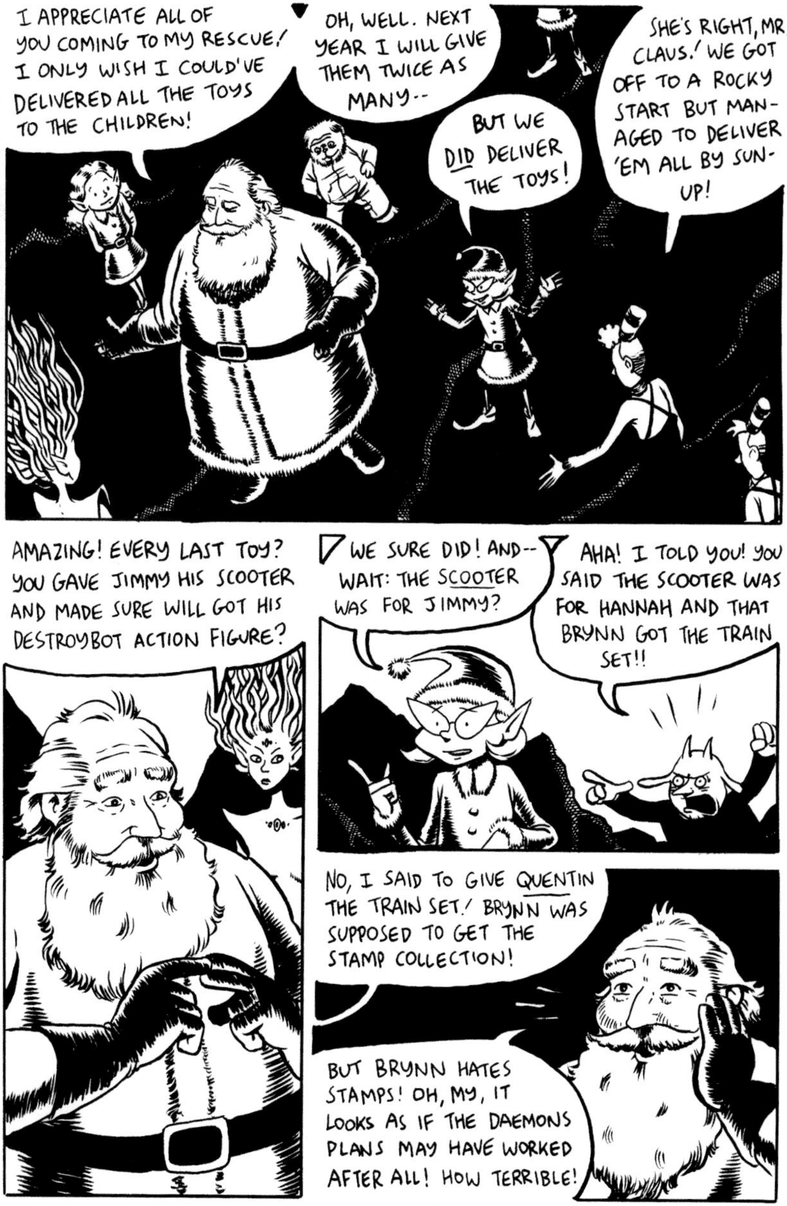
I APPRECIATE ALL OF YOU COMING TO MY RESCUE! I ONLY WISH I COULD'VE DELIVERED ALL THE TOYS TO THE CHILDREN!
OH, WELL. NEXT YEAR I WILL GIVE THEM TWICE AS MANY--
BUT WE DID DELIVER THE TOYS!
SHE'S RIGHT, MR. CLAUS! WE GOT OFF TO A ROCKY START BUT MANAGED TO DELIVER 'EM ALL BY SUN-UP!
AMAZING! EVERY LAST TOY? YOU GAVE JIMMY HIS SCOOTER AND MADE SURE WILL GOT HIS DESTROYBOT ACTION FIGURE?
WE SURE DID! AND-- WAIT: THE SCOOTER WAS FOR JIMMY?
AHA! I TOLD YOU! YOU SAID THE SCOOTER WAS FOR HANNAH AND THAT BRYNN GOT THE TRAIN SET!!
NO, I SAID TO GIVE QUENTIN THE TRAIN SET! BRYNN WAS SUPPOSED TO GET THE STAMP COLLECTION!
BUT BRYNN HATES STAMPS! OH, MY, IT LOOKS AS IF THE DAEMONS PLANS MAY HAVE WORKED AFTER ALL! HOW TERRIBLE!

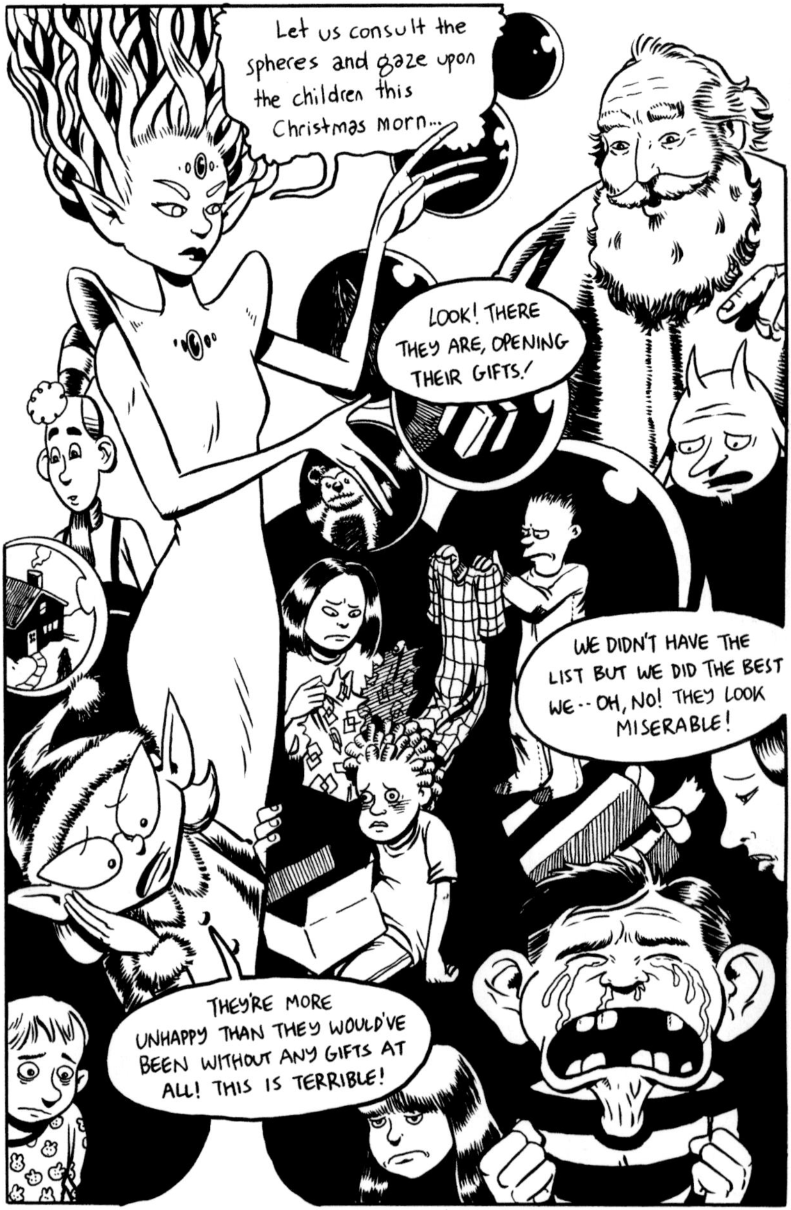
Let us consult the spheres and gaze upon the children this Christmas morn...
LOOK! THERE THEY ARE, OPENING THEIR GIFTS!
WE DIDN'T HAVE THE LIST BUT WE DID THE BEST WE-- OH, NO! THEY LOOK MISERABLE!
THEY'RE MORE UNHAPPY THAN THEY WOULD'VE BEEN WITHOUT ANY GIFTS AT ALL! THIS IS TERRIBLE!

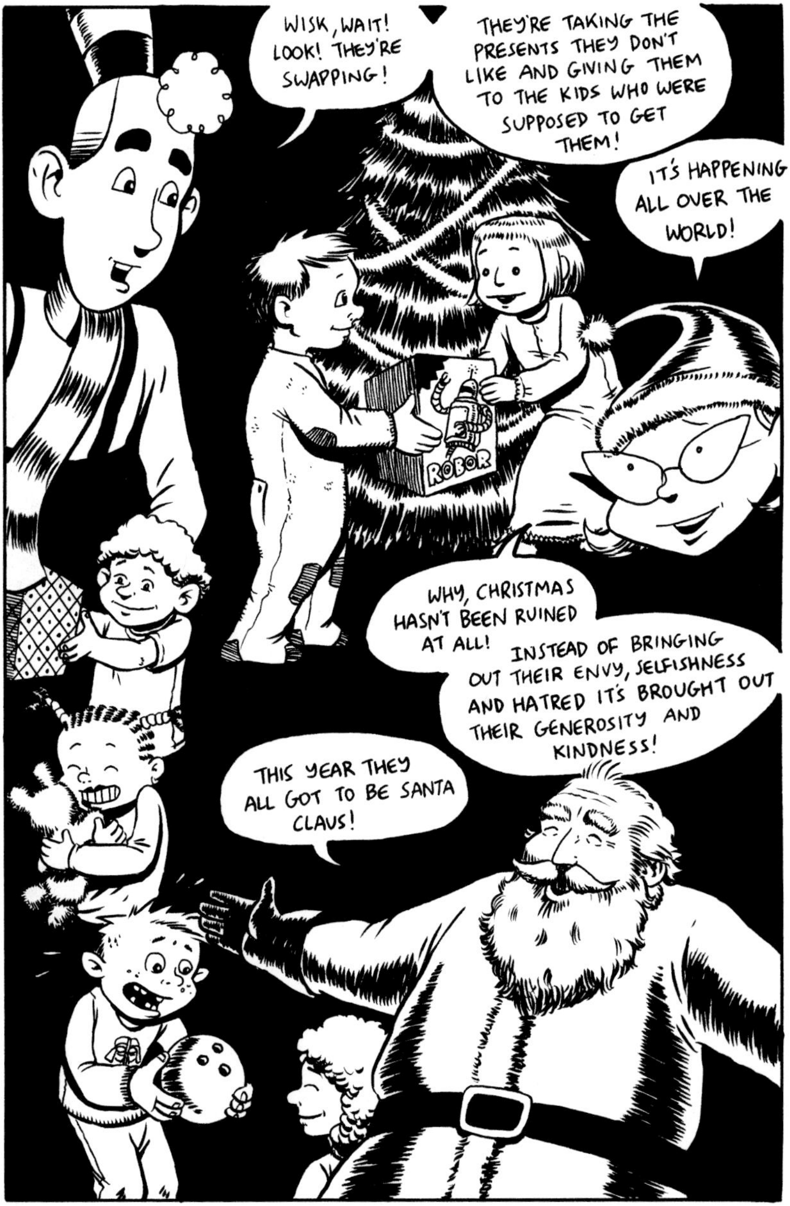
WISK, WAIT! LOOK! THEY'RE SWAPPING!
THEY'RE TAKING THE PRESENTS THEY DON'T LIKE AND GIVING THEM TO THE KIDS WHO WERE SUPPOSED TO GET THEM!
IT'S HAPPENING ALL OVER THE WORLD!
ROBOR
WHY, CHRISTMAS HASN'T BEEN RUINED AT ALL!
INSTEAD OF BRINGING OUT THEIR ENVY, SELFISHNESS AND HATRED IT'S BROUGHT OUT THEIR GENEROSITY AND KINDNESS!
THIS YEAR THEY ALL GOT TO BE SANTA CLAUS!

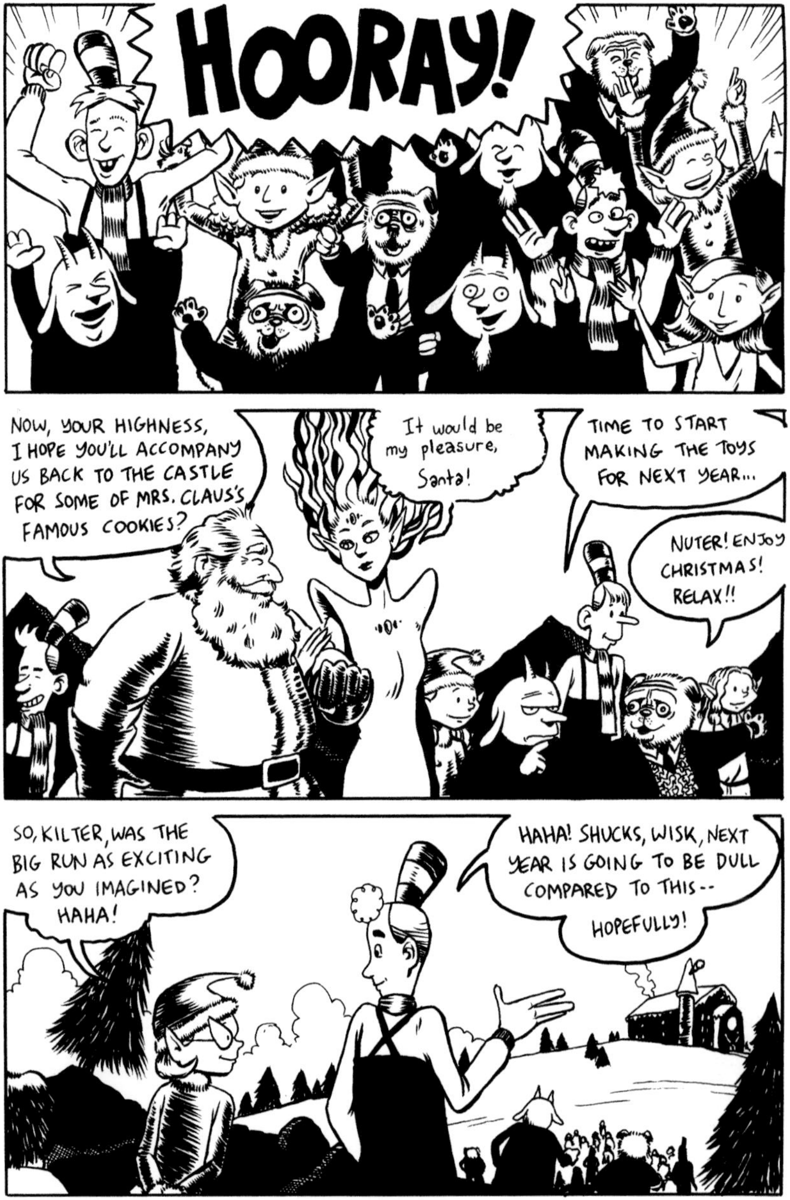
HOORAY!
NOW, YOUR HIGHNESS, I HOPE YOU'LL ACCOMPANY US BACK TO THE CASTLE FOR SOME OF MRS. CLAUS'S FAMOUS COOKIES?
It would be my pleasure, Santa!
TIME TO START MAKING THE TOYS FOR NEXT YEAR...
NUTER! ENJOY CHRISTMAS! RELAX!!
SO, KILTER, WAS THE BIG RUN AS EXCITING AS YOU IMAGINED? HAHA!
HAHA! SHUCKS, WISK, NEXT YEAR IS GOING TO BE DULL COMPARED TO THIS--
HOPEFULLY!

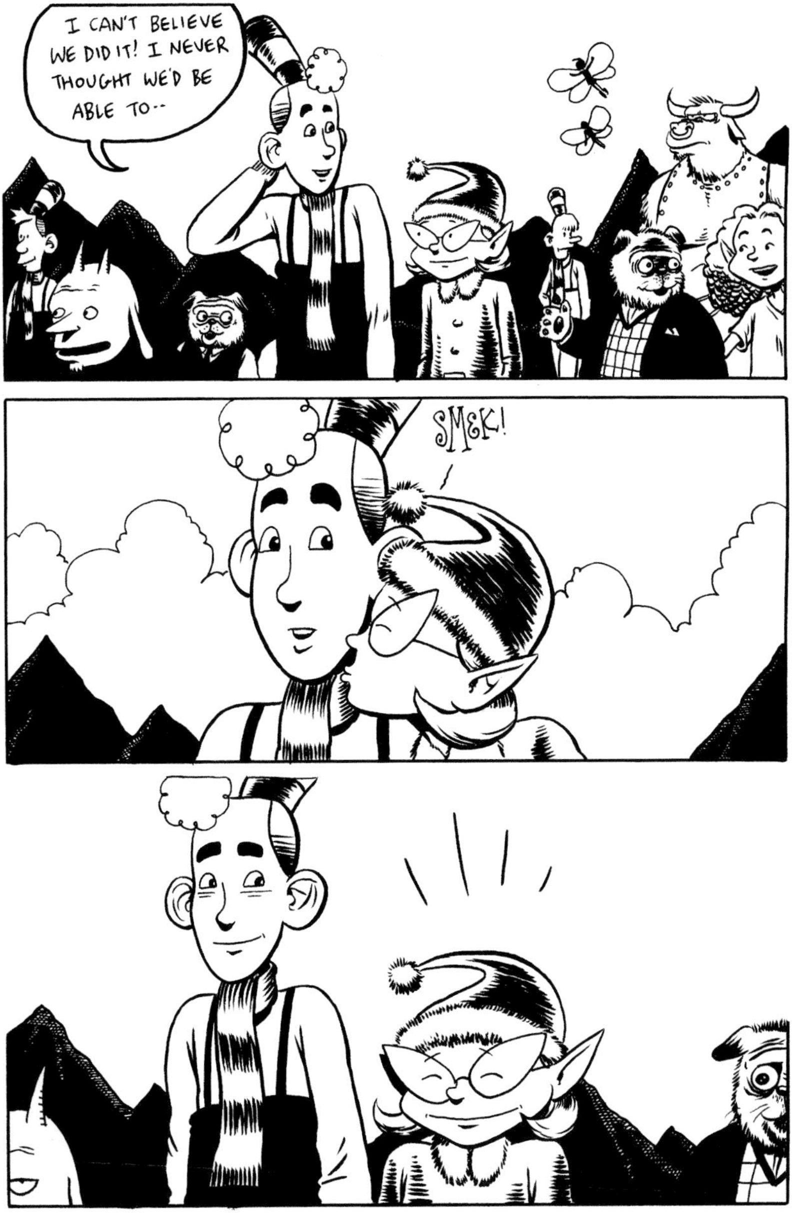
I CAN'T BELIEVE WE DID IT! I NEVER THOUGHT WE'D BE ABLE TO--
SMEK!

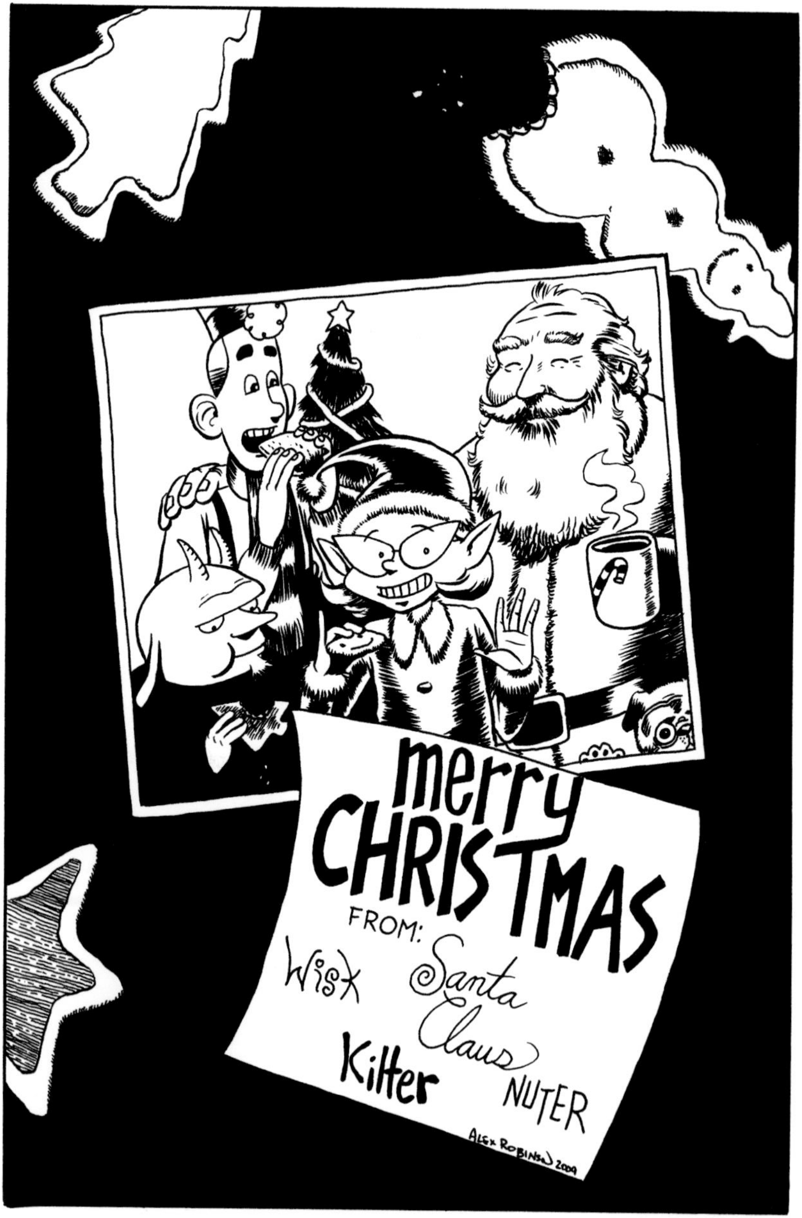
merry
CHRISTMAS
FROM:
Wisk
Santa Claus
Kilter
NUTER
ALEX ROBINSON 2009

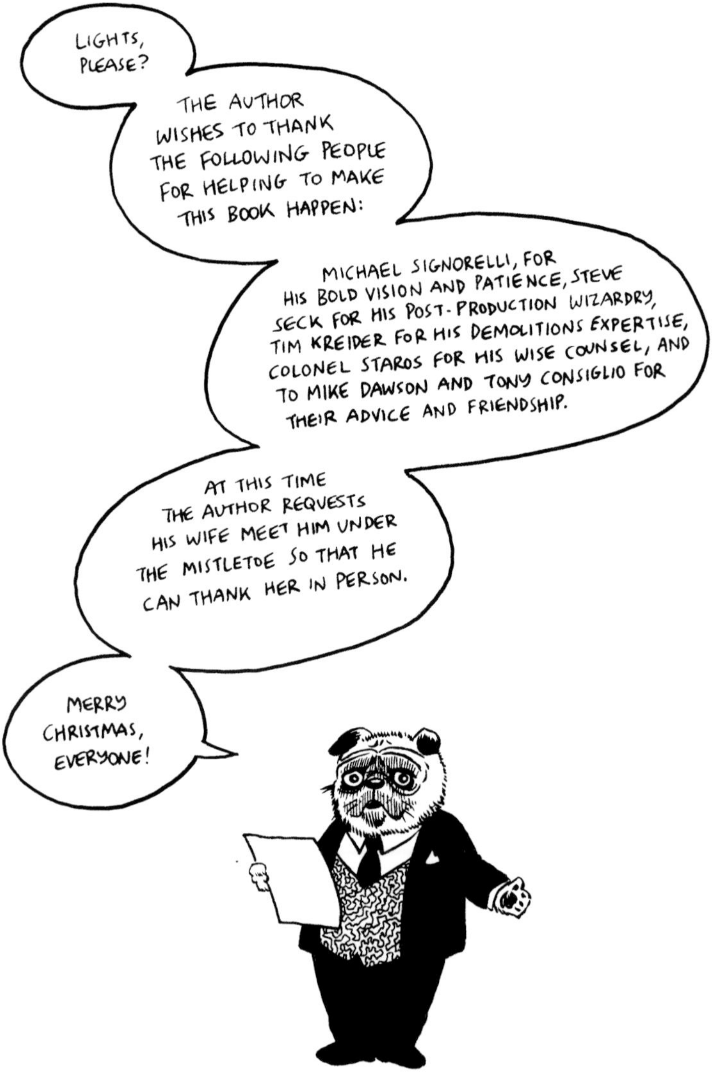
LIGHTS, PLEASE?
THE AUTHOR WISHES TO THANK THE FOLLOWING PEOPLE FOR HELPING TO MAKE THIS BOOK HAPPEN:
MICHAEL SIGNORELLI, FOR HIS BOLD VISION AND PATIENCE, STEVE SECK FOR HIS POST-PRODUCTION WIZARDRY, TIM KREIDER FOR HIS DEMOLITIONS EXPERTISE, COLONEL STAROS FOR HIS WISE COUNSEL, AND TO MIKE DAWSON AND TONY CONSIGLIO FOR THEIR ADVICE AND FRIENDSHIP.
AT THIS TIME THE AUTHOR REQUESTS HIS WIFE MEET HIM UNDER THE MISTLETOE SO THAT HE CAN THANK HER IN PERSON.
MERRY CHRISTMAS, EVERYONE!